Eat the Sky, Drink the Ocean

Eat the Sky, Drink the Ocean

edited by **Kirsty Murray,**
Payal Dhar, and **Anita Roy**

Margaret K. McElderry Books   New York London Toronto Sydney New Delhi

MARGARET K. McELDERRY BOOKS

An imprint of Simon & Schuster Children's Publishing Division

1230 Avenue of the Americas, New York, New York 10020

Contents

Introduction   vii

Cat Calls . . . . *Margo Lanagan*   i

Swallow the Moon . . . . *Kate Constable
and Priya Kuriyan*   ii

Little Red Suit . . . . *Justine Larbalestier*   29

Cooking Time . . . . *Anita Roy*   46

Anarkali . . . . *Annie Zaidi
and Mandy Ord*   58

Cast Out . . . . *Samhita Arni*   70

Weft . . . . *Alyssa Brugman*   84

The Wednesday Room . . . . *Kuzhali Manickavel
and Lily Mae Martin*   93

Cool . . . . *Manjula Padmanabhan*   103

Appetite . . . . *Amruta Patil*   113

Mirror Perfect . . . . *Kirsty Murray*   122

Arctic Light . . . . *Vandana Singh*   133

The Runners . . . . *Isobelle Carmody
and Prabha Mallya*   144

The Blooming . . . . *Manjula Padmanabhan
and Kirsty Murray*   156

What a Stone Can't Feel . . . . *Penni Russon*   167

Memory Lace . . . . *Payal Dhar*   180

Back Stage Pass . . . . *Nicki Greenberg*   190

Notes on the Collaborations   203

About the Contributors   219

Introduction

In late 2012, Australia and India were rocked by violent crimes against young women. In Delhi, thousands protested against rape. In Melbourne, thousands stood vigil in memory of a young woman raped and murdered while walking home. The fate of all young women, what they should fear and what they can hope for were hot topics in the media around the world. Out of that storm rose the idea for this anthology.

We decided on the title *Eat the Sky, Drink the Ocean* because it suggested impossibilities, dreams, ambitions, and a connection to something larger than humanity alone. It was inspired, in part, by a 1930s labor song in which bosses and priests tell workers that "You won't get to eat pie until you're in the sky" (i.e., until you're dead). "Pie in the sky" has come to mean any kind of wishful thinking—something you can't have in this lifetime.

This collection of stories embraces the idea of not just eating pie but of taking big, hungry mouthfuls of life and embracing the world. It's about the desire to have and do impossible things, especially things that girls aren't meant to do. We asked our contributors to reimagine the world, to mess with the boundaries of the possible and the probable.

Then we threw them another challenge. They were to work their magic in collaboration with a partner from the other country. Over Skype and e-mail they shared stories about the challenges of being a girl or woman, and speculated how the world could be otherwise. Our cross-border confabulations produced seventeen works of fiction—six graphic stories, one playscript, and ten short stories. In this collection you will find dystopian worlds and distant galaxies, alternative histories and time travel, fairy tales with a twist—and even a Shakespeare spinoff. You'd imagine a speculative feminist collection to be full of stories about strong and fantastic girls vaulting over traditional role barriers—but many of the stories are just as much about boys.

Some pairs worked together to craft a single piece of work, while others chose to bat ideas at each other and then work independently on a common theme. The notes at the end of the volume narrate their individual journeys; among the most interesting are the writer–illustrator pairs that started off skeptical and ended up sold on the idea of collaboration.

We wanted contributors to be bold, so we encouraged them to go beyond the expectations of their cultures, and to think not just about their own realities but also those of young adults, who may be like or unlike them. It was incredibly exciting to see people separated by thousands of kilometers sharing ideas about what it means to be human, to love and to live in this world. Unexpectedly, a strange synchronicity came into play. It was as if, unconsciously, the imaginations of all twenty artists and writers became interconnected.

Ultimately, this is a book about connections—between Australia and India, between men and women, between the past, the present, the future, and the planet that we all share. If we had to name one thing we learned in the process of making this anthology, it's the fact that when you eat the sky and drink the ocean, you are part of the Earth: everything's connected.

Cat Calls

Margo Lanagan

"But I *can't* whistle!" said Neddi. "My mouth is made wrong. I've tried and tried!"

"I can't whistle if I'm nervous." Shinna played with her fingers and glanced around. "Or if anyone's looking at me." We all looked away.

"I can't if I'm laughing," said Kate. A big grin burst out on her face. "And I just *know* I'll get the giggles, looking those fellows in the eye."

Dipti threw up her hands. "Well, dammit, we'll make a different noise. If you can't whistle, hiss! Everyone can hiss."

And they all hissed, like the sound of wind in dry grass.

I put my face in my hands. Dipti threw her hard, skinny arm around my shoulders and shook me. "Oh, if only I lived over the river!" I wailed. "Then my parents would buy me one of those Gran Sasso Devices, and I would be able to go wherever I wanted."

"It'd be wonderful, wouldn't it?" she said. "Just press the button and their filthy words fly right back into their mouths—never said, never heard."

"Why don't they just say them again, is what I don't understand?" said Shinna.

"It doesn't feel nice, Fan's sister says," said Kate, "having that little bit of time run backward, while the rest of it's running forward all around you. It feels like you're a sock, she says, being turned inside-out—because it's running *your* mind backward too. But it's better than being shouted at."

"Well, Melita." Dipti shook me again. "That kind of handy thing was never made for girls like us, was it? That's a weapon for rich men's daughters. And that's okay. We have no need of it—" She couldn't stop grinning. "Because we have a *plan*."

All the men were outside the teashop next morning. I felt sicker than ever with fear. Everything looked the same: the dusty road with not a soul on it, the closed-up church, the schoolhouse off in the distance. The air was still cool, and I was freshly bathed, and my clothes were crisp from laundering and drying in the sun, and there were the men all waiting, ready to attack. The big one leaned back in his chair. I had never seen him standing; perhaps he had *grown into* that straining chair, and sat there day and night? The two thin men lounged in the doorway, and Mr. Red Shirt and

Mr. Fancy Boots perched on the edges of the other chairs. They were talking now, but as soon as they saw me . . .

Just run past them. Ignore them, my mother had said. *The world is full of those men. They are not worth your time.*

Of course they call out to you, said my father. *They think you're beautiful. Which you are. And a beautiful young girl should be complimented.*

My mother had smacked his shoulder. *You don't know what you're talking about.* This made me feel hopeful for a moment—would she get angry enough to help me? But then my brothers had come home and my time for my parents' attention was over. *Take Otto's bags, Melita. Bring Charlie some tea.*

Walking closer to the teashop, I thought I saw a whisker of movement up near the church, but now as I stared, there was nothing. I was so confused—did I want my friends to be there or not? Had I been foolish to mention this, to say yes when Dipti offered to help? Would she make it better for me, or worse? Oh, whatever happened would be wrong and awful. I would be crushed and laughed at whether I was alone as usual or backed up by every girl in my class. These men, they didn't look like monsters, but the words pouring out of their mouths fouled up my whole world, every morning and every afternoon. Girls had no chance against it, young girls like us, from this side of town.

One of the thin men saw me and whistled. The other turned and stared, gave a little whooping noise. I stared at the church. Had they come? Oh, please! Oh, please *not!*

One head popped out, popped back behind the church

corner. Then two were quickly there and then gone. My heart lifted—and stuck in my throat for a moment, so that I couldn't breathe. I wanted just to run, to run up and meet my friends and tell them, *It's all right. They didn't say anything; there's no need for you to be here.* I could cope. I could be strong on my own.

The men began with their calling, with their crooning. Thin One and Thin Two got comfortable against the doorposts. Mr. Red Shirt sat forward in his chair. They threw out little remarks, soft and mocking, about my hair, my school uniform, my legs. If I'd been a rich girl, I'd have taken my little silver Gran Sasso Device out of my pocket right then, and pointed it at them—which would mean pointing it at myself, because it was a two-ended thing. And I would've pressed the blue button, and the particles faster than light, faster than time, would've burst out either end, and pulled those remarks out of my memory through my ears and folded them back down the men's throats. Of all the things scientists and corporations had found to do with neutrinos, the Gran Sasso was to me the greatest and the kindest. It was the one I could see a real use for, in my world, in my every day.

I was right in front of the shop now, and they were a chorus in my ear, gentle, awful, saying all their worst things, which they never got tired of calling out at me, at any girl who walked by on her own.

I stopped, my heart thudding so hard I was sure it would show, *ba-bump, ba-bump,* through my shirt. I turned to face them, which was my signal to the others, the one we'd agreed on. I stared boldly into the men's eyes, one after the other. I was sure they could see my fear, in my big eyes and my tight-pressed mouth.

The big man sneered and jerked his head at me. The thin men's grins stiffened on their faces. Mr. Red Shirt looked at the others to see what he should do, and Mr. Boots crooned on about what he might find under my uniform, then checked whether the big man approved. I didn't look away; I finished meeting all their eyes and went back to the big man and started again. My classmates were coming, my friends. First I heard their wolf-whistles, their *woo-hoos*, their hisses—then their shoes pattered on the dusty road.

I took one slow step, then another, toward the men. Thin One and Thin Two, they glanced up the road and looked actually afraid for a moment. I could hear it was a big crowd, bigger than Dipti had called together yesterday. There were boys' voices in it; boys had come too! Girls and boys pushed in behind and either side of me, and they whistled and hissed at the men.

Mr. Red Shirt laughed loudly. "All these girls for us! Some of them are pretty, too!"

I despaired at his confidence, and at the big man's easy way of sitting there. The other men would gather courage from it, I was sure, and hurl more words.

But Dipti got in before them. "Some of them are handsome, too!" she exclaimed, in exactly Mr. Red Shirt's tone.

"All these fellas for us! Aren't we lucky?" cried out a boy behind me.

"How about a kiss? Or just a smile?" someone else called coaxingly. "You'd be so pretty if you smiled."

And everyone else hissed and whistled.

"What do you think you're about, you kids!" Mr. Fancy Boots jumped up from his chair, and I flinched.

Someone put her hand on my shoulder and called, dreamily, "What do you think you're about?"

"What do you look like, without that uniform?" cried out a girl to Mr. Boots.

"Bring some of that over here!" That was Shinna.

"Yes, me and my friend would like a piece!" That girl could hardly speak for laughing.

"You're a hot little number!" said Dipti fiercely.

"Nice bottom, too!" someone piped up at the back. "See when he runs. Oh-*ho*! Bouncy-bouncy!"

"How about a kiss?"

And one by one they called out all the things the men had ever said, that I'd told them yesterday and Dipti had written down. Against a background of hoots and hisses they called them out. They chanted some of the sayings over and over, and they brought in new ones I was sure I hadn't told them, because I'd have been too embarrassed. They called out sayings I'd never heard myself, things these men had never said, words so foul I didn't know what they meant.

"That's enough!" shouted Thin Two. "You girls shouldn't talk like that."

"Girls shouldn't talk like that!" Dipti laughed.

But they did talk like that, all the girls behind me, and the one or two boys. They said all those embarrassing things. I said a few myself, a couple of the big man's suggestions— but I said them in that cool, dreamy way we were using, as if they were song-words or poem-words, or just interesting noises made by birds, or cats in the night, or elephants trumpeting. They filled the air all around, the words I'd tried to push out of my head so often, thinking that no other girl was tormented as I was. Everyone knew them—and some knew worse, so much worse! Everyone who'd heard them wanted to unhear them, to have them unsaid the way the Gran Sasso let you unsay them—but if we couldn't do that, the next best thing was to throw them back at the men with all their power gone out of them, like shucked-off snakeskins or dead balloons.

And the whistles and the hoots and the hisses—and some growls, even some dog barks!—they were like a nest made of sound. Inside that nest, I was protected right up to my ears. People who were too shy or scared to utter the horrible words, they could hiss; the hissing was a constant rushing all round me. The whistles were on different notes, and so were the calls—all the pretty-pretties and kiss-kisses and where's-your-lovely-smiles. It sounded beautiful, in a weird, wild way.

I felt like laughing, under cover of all our noise; I felt like crying, but I was too busy throwing ugly words back at the men. I didn't care what they did; it felt good to sing and shout out these things, from this big safe group. I could almost *understand* the men, why they did what they did. They must want this wonderful feeling. They must like being in *their* group, outside the teashop. Whatever horrible things they called out, it made sense that they too wanted to be among friends, gluing their group together better with every call.

The two thin men darted out at us. "Clear off! Get out of here with your dirty mouths, you filthy girls, shames of your mothers!"

We scattered backward, but no one stopped hissing or hooting, and Dipti stood firm and alone there. "Clear off!" she sang. "Get out of here!"

"Dirty mouths!" I called out as we hurried back to stand around her.

"Shames of your mothers!" said Neddi behind me.

"I'd like to look under that skirt," said a boy, and we laughed, because Thin Two had a sweater tied around his middle that did indeed flap like a skirt.

He stepped forward. He would have slapped Dipti, and she—she stood like a rock—she would have taken it, too.

But the big man spoke then. He just said Thin One's name, and that killed the fear in the man's eyes. How relieved he was, to have the big man take over! He spat, instead, at Dipti's feet. She hissed at him. "Filthy girls!" she caroled as he hurried back to his place at the door.

Then the big man moved. With his lip still curled at us, he hoisted his arms back to put his huge hands to the armrests of his chair; he unwedged himself from between them, and I saw that his tiny feet *could* take the full weight of him. He cast a last look over the crooning crowd behind me.

"Lovely pair of titties!" one of the boys called.

"Bring me some of that on a plate!" shouted Shinna.

And the big man turned his back on us, and Thin One and Thin Two stepped aside to let him enter the teashop door.

They swaggered and smirked, the Thins, and Red Shirt, and Boots, as they followed him in, but we had seen their fear, we had seen their doubt and confusion. They could swagger all they liked; *we* knew what they were. We had silenced them! We had made them get up and go inside!

The door closed behind them. Cheers went up among the hissing. Dipti waved our noise down. "I hereby declare, this road is safe for any girl to pass along!" And she came and hugged me.

"You are a wonderful friend." I hugged her back. Then Neddi joined in, and Suzy too, and someone else behind me, and everyone who was there, all laughing and holding tight. "*Everyone* is wonderful friends," I said, squashed in the middle. "All of you!"

Having sung us up the road to the school gate, the boys ran off to their school.

"Those men'll be there again tonight, of course," I said to Dipti. "Without you there, they will be just as rude as before."

Dipti burrowed in her pocket, brought out two folded pieces of lined paper and gave me one. Shinna and Kate waved their paper squares at me.

I unfolded mine. It was a neatly ruled table, filled out in Dipti's round handwriting. For each school day, she'd written the names of four of my classmates, two for morning, two for afternoon. And she'd put *Melita's Device* at the top, and drawn a Gran Sasso there with neutrinos spurting out both ends, each neutrino a star with a little *n* inside.

"I know," she said. "We are not a sweet, silver Device that

fits in the palm of your hand—we are a big, messy Device with lots of loose parts coming and going. But we don't cost anything, and we don't need a battery. And when we *do* work, we're much more fun."

The bell clanged, then, which was just as well, because my heart seemed stuck in my throat again, stopping me from speaking. I folded the paper, put it in my pocket, and ran after my friends into class.

Swallow the Moon
Kate Constable ∗ Priya Kuriyan

It's dark in the forest. We are all silent as we follow in the footsteps of the older women. We, the younger ones, don't know the way.

We have been walking since sunset, when our names were taken from us, and the light leached from the sky.

We should be tired, but fear and excitement drive us forward.

Each of us has been given a tiny bundle, wrapped in skin, and secret; we will not see inside until the moment of sacrifice. In a day and night of secrets, we know only this: when we have offered up these treasures, we will receive our new names. We will be fat with knowing, then.

The path is long, but our feet are light. The women begin to sing.

The dark stretches long;
the dawn is still far away.
The forest rings with the
call of a night bird.

We hear a sound we have never
heard before, but we recognize
it as surely as if it had been
woven through our dreams.
It is the bellow of the ocean,
like some great beast.

Far below, the ravenous waves devour the rocks, then, roaring, spit them out again.

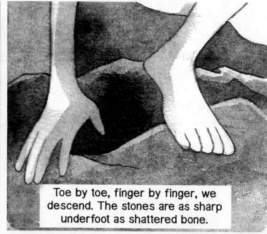

Toe by toe, finger by finger, we descend. The stones are as sharp underfoot as shattered bone.

At the water's edge we are timid before the hungry waves.

We wait.

One of the women crouches over the silver sand.

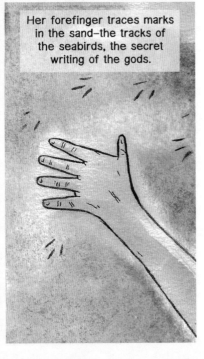

Her forefinger traces marks in the sand–the tracks of the seabirds, the secret writing of the gods.

At last she speaks. We have to listen hard; her words are scattered by the wind. She reads of our next few seasons, until the women come again to the shore with more young girls to be named. We smile, for we are to be lucky. The rains will fall, the plants will flourish, the sun will not burn too harshly.

The rest of us follow her, ungraceful, spluttering. We have swum in the river and the water hole, but never in the sea. We know we are not supposed to laugh, because this is a solemn night, but we are young, and light-headed with hunger, and the waves caress us.

We plunge our heads into that silver moontrail. We open our lips and take in a mouthful of that shining water, as warm and salty as our own blood.

It is not over. The women are waiting for us.

Clumsily, we paddle out to join them. We are just in time. The sky is a bowl of copper, a bowl of rosy gold, licked by the white flame of the rising sun.

When we reach them, the women dive. If we stay behind, we will be trapped in childhood, mired without a name.

We are gazing at a drowned city. A city of ancient times,
a city from Before, a city of warning and dread.
Once, birds flew through the canyons of these streets.
Now we glide above, struck silent with awe.

The women gather us, high above the dead city.
We uncurl our hands, and look at last, solemn and reverent,
at the little objects we have carried so far.

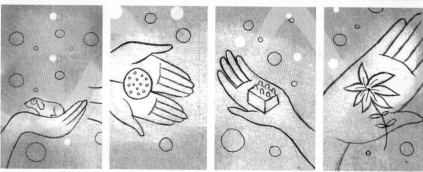

It cost so much to produce these sacred treasures—in oil, in energy burned,
in forests destroyed. These things must have been much loved, and filled
with power, to be worth the sacrifice of a whole world.

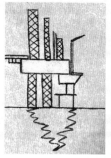

BERRDA..

We learn our new names.

We must not linger. We hold out our hands. And we let go.

Tumbling noiselessly, the precious, weighted objects fall.

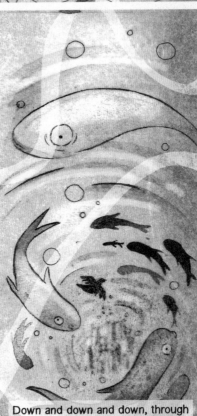

Down and down and down, through the cloudy green of the sea, they spin into the yawning jaws of the street-trenches. Our childhoods, our former names, our past selves, are all digested in the belly of Before.

We stumble back onto the patch of sand and scramble again up the path. We have to help one another, and we understand that this is all part of the lessons of the day.

We turn our backs on the dazzling sea and its mysteries. We fold our secrets inside our hearts; they are part of us now. Once more, we face the forest's shadows.

When we arrive home, back among the men, we will tell our new names aloud. For now they lie inside our closed mouths. As we walk, holding our names unspoken, we are becoming new women.

At the end of the line, Berrda drifts into dreaming.

All at once, she is alone.

She is not supposed to call; we are meant to keep silent, until we open our mouths to let our new names flutter free. All she can hear are the indifferent birds, flitting unseen above.

Drawn back to the sound of the sea, she emerges from the forest again. But this time, she is not on the cliff top.

There is no sand here on which the birds can leave their messages from the gods.

The beach is blanketed with rags and rinds of plastic, blue and white and yellow, pink and lime and tangerine.

Slowly she begins to understand.

The women come here, secretly, to find the trinkets from Before. One day, we will come here too. We will lead the trek through the forest, and read the messages in the birds' tracks. We will teach the young girls how to dive, and show them the drowned city at the bottom of the sea. It will be us, mothers and grandmothers and aunts by then, who will search for small treasures for the girls to hold, on the night they swallow the moon.

And at last, she hears the call from the forest, from someone come to find her. A cloud of birds flies up, pouring into the sky, as if all the small objects and all our secrets and all our fears were suddenly let go.

Little Red Suit

Justine Larbalestier

For my favorite engineer, Varian Johnson

You've heard this story. Only this time she didn't meet a wolf in the woods. There were no woods, no wolves.

Besides, everyone knows men are worse than wolves. Sharper teeth too.

The only thing that was the same was the redness: the suit she wore was scarlet.

The knife she wielded was sharp.

Her name was Poppy.

Poppy was fifteen years old and had never seen rain. The drought began six years before her birth. The longest on record.

She was born in Sydney, that city of fewer than fifty

thousand souls existing in protective suits underground, beneath precarious shielding, on islands that had once, before the seas rose, been part of the mainland. The city had had seasons once. Now it was drought for years and years, or floods and then years of drought again.

So many years that Poppy didn't quite believe in rain.

Her Grandma Lily refused to live in the city. She was one of the folk who lived in sealed homes outside the city. She contributed to the city and in turn the city supported her. Every year there were fewer like her.

Grandma refused to move from the home that had been the family's since the 1880s, when trees could live outside, and sun and wind and rain didn't kill everything.

Killed almost everything, but not hard-shelled insects, not bacteria.

Her grandmother said she could fix what needed fixing. She was an engineer. The shielding had mostly failed, the neighborhood been abandoned; Grandma's house, even with all her fixes, would be uninhabitable soon.

Grandma Lily hadn't replied to Poppy's last message. But Grandma often skipped mail for days, saving electricity to reduce the heat.

Poppy knew she was alive, but her mum had decided Grandma was gone. Poppy closed her eyes, breathed deep, let a tear roll down her cheek, before the moisture was reabsorbed into her suit with only a trace of salt left.

Poppy's mum didn't understand Grandma Lily; she wasn't an engineer. But Poppy and her grandmother were the same kind: she was going to be an engineer too.

She messaged Grandma Lily again.

Poppy was desperate to see her, desperate, too, to get out of the city, where she lived pressed too close to people whose faces she'd tired of. Poppy wanted to walk without being jostled, propositioned, or pawed—it was always the same creeps, the unassailable doctors, teachers, lordly engineers—or admonished, or given work she didn't want to do, or lectures on how they had to pull together if she showed any reluctance to do that random work.

She was sick of the two-meter-by-two-meter room she shared with her mother, where it was hard not to think of the tons of earth, and concrete, and other people's homes pressing down on her. Where the walls were so thin that signing was the only way to communicate privately.

She wanted to see the moon and the stars through less than six or seven layers.

If Poppy couldn't escape—even for a day—she'd explode.

There was no prison in the city. If you ran amok you were put outside, without a suit. Two weeks ago an engineer had tried to force himself on an apprentice, not caring that there were dozens of witnesses. The city put him outside.

No one left the city alone on foot unless it was punishment. Or suicide. There were rumors of people living out there wild. Poppy didn't believe it.

She would have to walk to her grandmother's. They couldn't afford to hire a car, and public transport only ran during the day. All battery-stored energy was saved for hospitals and lowering the temperature at night.

Solar and wind power was all there was.

There and back was only a two-hour journey. She had done it before with her mum.

This time her mum would not join her.

They fought.

Her mother tried to reason with her, tried blackmail, threats. She didn't raise her voice. No one ever did; eventually the ones who yelled walked out of the city without a suit.

Her Uncle Jon wished to see her. Poppy shook her head.

We owe him, her mother signed.

No, you owe him, Poppy didn't sign.

Her mother's best friend, Ana, nodded. *It's politic to see him.*

Poppy felt the weight of their disapproval.

Their suits hung from pegs on the wall. Ana's was yellow. The new suits were yellow or white or silver, to reflect light, not absorb it. Imported from India. Everything good came from there or the Americas.

Poppy went to see him. He wasn't her real uncle. Her mother and he had been friends when they were little. Then he became an engineer; she didn't. Her mother owed him and owed him until now he owned her.

But he doesn't own me, Poppy also didn't sign. No one was ever going to own her.

She agreed to meet him in Whitlam Square with her suit on and hundreds jostling them. The shielding there was good—eight layers—the air mostly breathable.

He was on the Council. A respected man. A popular,

handsome man. Everyone said so. Everyone nodded and smiled at him as they went by.

Poppy and Uncle Jon unsealed their visors so they could speak unmonitored. Signing wasn't private in public. Uncle Jon's suit was silver, the most expensive kind.

"There are monsters out there," he said. She could barely hear him over the crowd. She did not lean closer.

"I'll be careful," Poppy said, not believing him. Nothing could live out there, not without a suit, not without support from the city.

"You might not come back," he said, sealing his visor, walking away.

She wondered why anyone thought him handsome.

Even Poppy's best friend, Umami, thought she was an idiot.

Not that I don't long to be somewhere else. But there is nowhere else. Until we're engineers. It's the only here we've got.

Umami was an apprentice too. It was what anyone smart did.

Leaving the city alone on foot, even in a suit, was not.

They sat on top of the craft hall, in their suits— Umami's was green, old, but not so old as Poppy's— looking east at what had been Sydney. Most of it under water, except these few islands. Her grandmother on one of the closer ones.

They weren't alone—they were never alone—but there were fewer people on this roof. Unbreathable air.

Is that a crack? Umami pointed to a fissure forming in the shielding.

Poppy nodded. There were too many cracks. Umami signed that she was reporting it. It would be added to the list.

They might not let you go.

I'm fifteen. They have to.

We'll get to the Americas, or India, Umami signed.

The only places you could walk outside at night without a suit.

You and me. We'll sit their exams and they'll whisk us away.

It had been years since anyone from Sydney had managed it. Uncle Jon had failed five times.

I'll be a chemical engineer and you mechanical.

In the city, engineers didn't specialize. They had to do everything; so nothing was done well. Grandma Lily's words, but Poppy knew it was true.

Did you hear some of the engineers have been getting exiled on purpose? They're building a secret city.

I roll my eyes, Poppy signed, without actually rolling them. Those rumors had been around for years. Umami believed the most unlikely tales. *Can you imagine? All those nasties building a hidden city? They'd kill each other in a week.*

I guess, Umami signed. *Be careful.*

Everyone knew everyone's business. They flicked their hands in disapproval when Poppy passed them in the halls. She stopped taking calls. She was fifteen; she didn't need permission.

Out loud her mother said, "You are reckless. You are wrong."

They always signed. Poppy could hear the neighbors agreeing. They, too, wanted everyone to hear.

Her mother's words made her stomach tight.

Then her mother turned her back, did not sign, or say, another word.

Three days of silence.

Poppy felt cold.

She left without her mother's approval.

Poppy stepped through the final seal of the city, as the last traces of sun disappeared, leaving behind disapproving looks, people pressed too close. She crossed the cleared perimeter quickly—it felt too exposed—much better to be in the remains of the old city, amidst semifossilized trees, crumbling buildings, and piles of rubble.

She walked along with her arms stretched out, not touching anyone. She couldn't see anyone. Poppy smiled.

Once it had been a tree-lined street. She'd never seen it that way, nor had her grandmother, yet Poppy knew how it had been. Everyone did. The city was dedicated to keeping memories of the old city alive.

These trees had been purple in the spring, green throughout the summer, shading the street, the footpath, the rows of terrace houses.

Now they were dead, what had been footpath was dirt and gravel, indistinguishable from the street, and most of the houses were gone. At the coolest time of year, in the dark, the city sent out teams to shore up the buildings marked for preservation.

Poppy felt a curious scratching between her shoulder blades as if someone were watching her. She turned. All she saw were scattered lights from the city's hospitals.

A beetle scuttled over her suited foot. She lit up her right palm: black and red shell, yellow body. Plague beetle. They ate everything: plants, other insects, anything decomposing.

Some tried to eat the fossilized trees.

Long ago it had been bad luck to see a plague beetle. Now they were everywhere, a few even made it into the city. Poppy figured that meant they were all doomed: living mostly underground, in an inadequately shielded city, on strict rations and never enough water, far from India, from the Americas, from the places that were more than merely surviving.

Poppy quickened her pace, saw another beetle, crunched it underfoot. She smiled. Plague beetles were why so many greenhouses had been abandoned. She felt good killing them.

Her mother said every life was sacred; Poppy didn't agree.

Her shoulder blades still prickled. She turned. Saw nothing. If her suit were newer, her screen would show her behind, above too.

What if there was a secret dwelling of survivors? They'd prey on anyone foolish enough to leave the city alone, wouldn't they?

She heard what sounded like a howl. Couldn't be the wind; there was no wind. She turned slowly. The moon was bright enough to produce shadows, but the shadows were of dead trees, dilapidated buildings. Something flickered in the distance.

The sky broke open with a thousand jagged shards of light. Something boomed. Poppy raised her suited hands to her suited ears. It sounded like an explosion. But she saw no fire.

Thunder. Lightning. An electrical storm.

There'd been no warning. Even now as the thunder crashed, her suit gave no weather warnings.

A call pinged. Her mother. Poppy was half tempted not to take it.

"Hello," Poppy said at last.

"The lightning is too close. Come home."

"I thought you weren't talking to me." Poppy could hear the whine in her own voice and wished she could take her words back.

"An electrical storm is dangerous."

Poppy couldn't argue with that. She walked closer to the buildings while quickening her pace so her mother could see on her screen that Poppy wasn't turning around. She took a sip from her suit, just back from its checkup, cleaner, and recycling water and air better than it had in months. The water tasted almost sweet. That would change.

The thunder crashed again, so close, so loud, the ground beneath her feet shifted, she tripped, landed heavily in the loose dirt. Her feet sliding on gravel, the weight of her pack pulling her backward.

Poppy heard something rip.

Felt heat, burning. Her suit, her back, at the lower ribs, just below her pack, exposed to air.

She leaped up, ignoring pain, walking faster, groping for her pack. She had to fix the tear. She had to keep moving.

If she stopped, the beetles, and who knew what nasty bacteria, would get in through the tear, into where her skin was burning.

"What is it, Poppy?"

Poppy wished she hadn't taken the call. "Nothing. Tripped. Distracted by talking to you. I'll call again when I get to Grandma's."

She clicked off before her mother could respond.

Poppy opened her pack, pulled out tape, patches, twisting to place a patch on her back, to tape it in place. The tape twisted, stuck to itself. There wasn't much left. She pried it apart, slowly, patiently, while still walking, while her back burned, while she ignored her mother calling. She sipped more water trying to stay calm.

She kept moving, eyes on the tape in her suited hands, shifting her gaze occasionally, to glance at the ground.

Tape separated, she twisted to run it along the edge of the patch leaving no gaps, to make sure it was in place over where it burned. Her sweat ran salt into the burning. She didn't scream. She hadn't since she was three years old.

The patch in place, pressing hard along the tape, forcing it to adhere. Miracle tape. She'd made condensation traps out of it. Grandma said you could build a spaceship from it.

Another crash of thunder, shaking the ground. Poppy tripped but did not fall. Her shoulder blades still itched. Someone couldn't be following her. She would've seen them. She was almost at the end of the island, if she turned back now . . . Poppy could hear her mother's told-you-sos. Dry storms always passed quickly.

It felt like the patch was in place. It had to be. If she'd had a better suit . . .

Poppy didn't know how many layers of skin she'd lost. Wouldn't know till she returned, pointless thinking about it.

She passed the Yellow House. Seven stories tall. No one knew now what it had been. Or why it was called that. If it had ever been yellow it was a long time ago.

The ground started to slope. The water wasn't far now.

Poppy heard howling.

Not her imagination.

It couldn't be a wolf. Though that's what it sounded like. She'd seen vids of them. Yellow eyes, strong jaws. There'd never been any here. Dingoes, long ago. Even longer ago, marsupial lions. Those were the only things that had howled here. No mammals, no reptiles, very few species could survive on this scorched earth, under this hot sun, with these poisons in the air and in the soil. Only humans found ways to eke out a kind of survival.

The howl had to be a recording.

Poppy walked faster.

I can help you with that.

Poppy spun around. There was no one.

The voice was inside her suit.

She felt chilled. She hadn't heard a ping, hadn't accepted a call. The caller had no ID. Someone had hacked her suit.

She shut off the call.

I can make sure your suit is patched securely.

She blocked the call.

I can get you to your grandmother's house.

Nothing worked.

"Who is this?"

Someone who can help you.

She was sure she'd heard that voice before.

The howling again. A human wolf.

I can get you to your grandma's house.

Shut up, she didn't say.

More thunder, more lightning.

Jagged lights across the water. The sea. Calm and low tide.

Two boats left. Both marked as seaworthy. People were careful to wipe those marks off when a boat started to take in water and they didn't have time to repair it. The few who lived out here depended on the boats being well maintained.

Poppy set the oars in place, looked around one more time. Whoever the mysterious caller was they were not in sight. They were probably back in the city. Playing games.

She rowed toward her grandma's island, ignoring the pain of her back, the feeling of being watched.

Hard and fast, she rowed, finding her rhythm. She would get to Grandma Lily.

Her mother called again.

Poppy ignored her.

I can fix your suit, the voice said. *Get you to her quickly, safely. Then home. No charge. No debt.*

She tried to shut the call off.

I'd like to help you. I like you.

The voice buzzed in her ears, making her wish she could wash. When she reached her grandma she'd scrape herself clean.

As she approached the shore she heard the howling again.

She sipped at her suit. Only the barest trickle. That wasn't right. She sipped again. Mere drops.

She'd fallen once. Surely that couldn't have damaged the recycling function? Her suit was old but solid. She'd fallen a million times, been banged into even more. The suit had just been repaired.

She was almost there now. In an emergency she could always call a courier. Or Emergency Services.

A real emergency. Not a bit of lightning and thunder, and some creepy prankster hacking her suit's communications.

She splashed through the shallow waters, pulling the boat high onto the shore. Laying the oars inside. Her back burned, but she didn't think it was worse. Patch was holding.

A howl surrounded her as she moved up the beach. As if the animal—it couldn't be an animal—was right there. She spun. Nothing.

More sweat. Fear sweat.

She took an involuntary sip. Almost nothing. But all that sweat? Should be a steady flow of water. Was the suit clogged?

I can help you anytime, darling.

She almost told him where to go.

Instead she called ES. "I'd like to report a hack. Someone's talking to me without permission, without ID."

The operator put Poppy on hold, which meant she was low priority. She wasn't an engineer yet. Her mother wasn't important. She'd voluntarily left the city. It was only a hack.

41

Poppy called her mother to tell her what was happening so her mum didn't hear it from someone else. The speed of gossip was faster than the speed of light.

"Just a prank," she told her. "No need to worry. Almost at Grandma's." She cut her off before she could I-told-you-so Poppy to death.

They won't help, the voice told her. *They can't track me. You won't get to your grandma before I do.*

She was still on hold. Maybe the operator was already monitoring these calls.

That howl. Again.

Poppy barely kept her scream inside.

She ran. She didn't care if whoever it was could see her speeding up. That they knew they'd rattled her. She would get to Grandma.

Her mother called. She ignored it.

You can't hide. Your suit is red. It pops. Like blood on snow.

Poppy had never seen snow. No one she knew had.

A lightning strike too close by. More thunder. In the same direction as her grandma's.

Sky's on fire. Is that your grandma's house?

Poppy ran faster, dirt kicking up. Old streetlights protruding from what had been the road, offering no light, plastic and wires long since stripped away. More dead trees. Power poles with no wires, connecting nothing to nothing.

Then, at the top of the hill, her grandma's house. The only house not in ruins.

She almost shouted, *Yes!*

But lightning flashed. The front of the house momentarily visible as day. Then back to moonlight.

It was enough.

Poppy had seen her grandma. Grandma Lily wouldn't be coming back to the city. She wouldn't be saying good-bye.

The house's seal was broken.

Grandma Lily was on the remains of the porch, leaning on the railing.

Without her suit.

Dried-out eyes open, skin turned leather, hair gone.

Grandma Lily had long white hair she wore in a bun. She never wore her suit inside, only out. No matter how hot it got. That's how Poppy knew the color and texture and smell of her grandma's hair. The hair that was gone.

Every window was broken. The porch glittered with shards of glass.

The seal wasn't just broken; it was shredded.

Should've told you it was too late, shouldn't I?

Poppy ran into the house, grabbed everything that wasn't destroyed. Books had disintegrated, most of the plastics melted, but some of Grandma's hardware was locked away. Poppy put as much as she could into her pack. Grandma's knife too. She'd designed it herself, could cut through anything. Totally illegal.

No tears for Grandma Lily, only burning eyes.

Poppy sipped again. No water at all.

She checked her grandma's condensation traps, the ones she'd helped her build. Poppy attached her suit, extracted all the H_2O she could.

The sky cracked open. Thunder, lightning, at the same time. Her ears echoed with it. The afterimage played across her eyes.

Time to leave.

She paused on the steps, looking at Grandma Lily, wishing she could touch her. Skin to skin. One last time.

A howl filled the air.

Water fell from the sky. Giant drops bounced back from the unshielded steps.

Rain.

It fell loud and fast.

Rain.

It's rain, the voice told her helpfully. *You're too young to have seen it before.*

Poppy called ES and told them about Grandma Lily.

"Your situation is being monitored," a different operator said. "Are you requesting extraction?"

It would cost too much.

In her suit she heard laughter. Only children laughed; by the time you were ten you'd learned to turn laughter off, or transform it into a smile.

"Are you requesting extraction?"

"No."

Her mother called.

"On my way," Poppy told her. "Grandma's dead."

Poppy felt her throat tighten. She clicked off before her mother could say anything.

Let me take you home, Poppy. In your little red suit.

"No," she said. "You're not even here."

She was afraid. Her mouth was dry. She didn't sip, wanting to make the water last.

The rain unceasing. If she could take off her visor, drink it in.

I am here.

Poppy spun around. Something was moving in the house.

She slid her hand into her pack, found the razor-sharp knife, unsheathed it, keeping her eyes on whatever was in Grandma Lily's. She tried to get through to ES. "I'm being attacked," she told their message bank.

Someone grabbed her from behind. She slashed with her knife. Twisting to get away.

She felt something tear. Her knife through a suit, tearing through as she leaned away, almost losing her grip.

The person let go, tumbled down the steps. Howled.

Not a wolf. A man in a suit.

She held her grandmother's knife out to the rain, watched the blood wash away, headed back to the city.

Cooking Time
Anita Roy

The minute the doorbell rang, I knew that something was wrong. The sound set my nerves jangling, as if it was plugged into my brain. My thoughts flew to the box in the basement, but before I could move, Marra had leaped up. "That will be Mandy," she said. "About time too." She opened the door. Two men stood in the street. They had AgroGlobal written all over them: dark suits, short hair, clean shoes, mirrored shades.

"We're looking for Miss Stella Jordan?" the first one said.

Marra looked back at me, worry in her dark eyes.

"You need to come with us," he said.

I got up. "Can I just . . ."

"Now."

There was no use protesting. I grabbed my bag and headed out.

There was a silver van standing outside. It looked so out of place in our street: like platinum dentures in a vagrant's ruined mouth. "Nice wheels," I said. Suit One gave a small, tight smile as he held open the door.

"Where are you taking me?" I asked as we pulled out. We drove past crumbling buildings and old iron staircases, bumping over potholes.

"Nothing to worry about," he said.

That wasn't an answer, but it didn't matter: I knew anyway. There was nowhere in Sector 87 to go, except for AgroGlobal.

At that moment, all I felt was angry. I'd always known that Mandy's obsession would get us into trouble. But would she listen? Never. She would just get that look on her face, biting her lip, her eyebrows drawn together in a line.

"I'm going to win, Stella," she would say to me. "I know I can cook."

The weird thing is, she could, you know? She really knew how to cook. Nobody from the Sectors had even *seen* real food in their lifetime. It was fifty years since the Dying Out, thirty since the last of the great food wars, and twenty since AgroGlobal crushed the last aquaculture smallholdings, and established itself as the world's largest—only—manufacturer of artificial food. "Newtrition" they called it, which quickly got shortened to "Newtri." "*Newtri: Fueling the Future,*" the ads say. "With over 70 great flavors to choose from, just squeeze and go!" No mess, no fuss, and, although I'd like to say no hunger, at least people no longer starved to death. We owed everything to AgroGlobal—and they owned everything. Governments, armies, energy production, manufacturing, media, health care, communications, travel—temporal and spatial—you name it, they owned it. Everything needed people, and people needed fuel, and we all needed Newtri. That's not to say that everyone was happy about it—I mean, look around you, right? But what choice did we have?

We all grew up on Newtri. Marra said us younglings were always clamoring for our tubes, but Mandy? She'd have just faded away if Marra hadn't practically injected it into her. She was always the littlest of us; still is. We used to call her "2D"—turn her sideways and she'd vanish. I always had to remind her to fuel up. "Yum, roast chicken and beans, and apple crumble. Your favorite," I'd say. She'd suck up a bit of her Newtri and then hand the rest to me while Marra wasn't looking. I wasn't complaining.

The driver took a right turn out of the Sector and onto the highway. I looked out at the dusty, ravaged land that stretched away on either side till it merged with the horizon, and thought back to that day two years ago when AgroGlobal TV had announced that the online Temporal Relocation Portal had gone live, and that the biggest show on the planet was about to be broadcast: MasterChef of All Time.

That was the day everything stopped. Schools closed, offices shut down, factories were silent—the skyways were empty, there wasn't a single auto on the streets. Everyone was home watching.

It was the reality show to end all reality shows. Twelve specially selected contestants were sent back in time to battle it out every week for the ultimate prize: the MasterChef Golden Apron. In the words of Judge Cheng, "We're not just talking real food, we're talking about real cooking—you gotta work for it. You want to make fish? You got to catch the bugger first. You want to roast potatoes? You got to dig 'em up. You gotta chop your logs and stoke up that fire before you even *think* about baking. You get me?"

It was a seriously great show. We all loved it; everyone did! But Mandy? She didn't just love it, she was obsessed— she was *addicted*. She'd stare at the screen as if she was eating it with her eyes. She used to record every episode, and play it back in slo-mo, freeze-framing, and all the time scribbling away. There were stacks of notebooks and scraps of paper in her room. "Recipes?" I said to her. "I mean, *recipes*? Seriously? What's the point of recipes if you got no fragging *ingredients*?" And she'd give me that look again. It was like talking to a wall.

One day, we were sitting on the bed waiting for the show to start. I always got that fluttery feeling in my tummy when the music came on, and they showed those clips of contestants in past episodes cooking away all over the place: quail consommé in Victorian England, ragi parathas in Harappa, an entire medieval banquet with roast suckling pig and sweet potatoes, and those *langues de chat* and petits fours in a Parisian salon. It was that episode when they went back to ancient Crete and had a pressure test for calamari dolmas on a bed of rocket and cilantro salad, and at the end of it, Mandy turned to me and said—and I remember this clearly, 'cause it was just the weirdest sentence I'd ever heard—"I would have caramelized squid ink for the vinaigrette." I just looked at her. "What? It would totally bring out the feta," she said, as if I was the idiot.

When the show was over, Mandy took me by the hand and stood up. "There's something I want to show you," she said. I followed her out of the room and down the stairs to the basement. She moved a pile of broken-down crates, and reached behind the pipes to bring out a battered old box. It had a long wooden handle, and the flaps on top hinged open showing neat drawers stacked on top of each other. Inside were an assortment of knives, metal spoons, a long, cylindrical thing made of wood, a pair of what looked like pliers with wire mesh at the ends, and all sorts of other stuff. "My tools," she whispered. Then she took my hand and held it really hard. "Stella, I've put my name in for the tryouts."

I really thought she'd lost it. Okay, so she had somehow—God alone knows how—managed to collect all these bits and pieces of junk, and she'd read just about everything she could lay her hands on about cooking, but that was all just *theory*! All the other contestants, in the whole history of MasterChef, had been from the Elites. People who had money and resources—some of them even (so people said) had *kitchens*, not that they had much to do in them but play around with different blends of Newtri, but still. They came from a different world. She didn't stand a chance.

I was so wrong.

She *aced* the tryouts. At fifteen, Mandira became not only the youngest contestant to compete on MasterChef, but the only one ever who wasn't an Elite. Imagine, one of us, a girl from humble old Sector 87 up there on screen for all the world to see. Everyone went crazy. "Mandira the Marvel!" the headlines screamed. "Teen Cooks Her Way Into History!!" Mandy became a star overnight.

She came back after a month, and she was *glowing*. Seriously! She literally couldn't stop talking about all the food that she'd eaten: "Oh my God, Stella," she'd say, "the *peas*. You pick them like this"—she pinched her fingers together and twisted—"and then pop the pods"—she flicked her thumb and index finger together—"and just eat them straight, and . . . oh . . . they were soooo . . ." And she'd put her fingers on her lips like she was remembering the sweetest kiss, and she'd be lost for words.

A month later, the day the first round was broadcast, practically the whole block came over to watch. You should have seen her prep that halibut! Most people haven't even *seen* a fish—not outside Planet Ocean Aquarium anyway—but she had that fish deboned and on the slab as if she was born with a—what did she call it?—a lithium-ion fillet knife in her hand. What a party we had that night! And the week after, and the week after that, until all the contestants had been eliminated, one by one, and it was down to the final three: Jerome with the floppy hair, Sherna the big-boned girl from Sector 47, and our Mandira.

When she left early this morning for the shoot, she seemed a little distracted, I guess. I put it down to nerves—I mean, even Mandy has gotta get nerves—but now I'm not so sure. Before she left, she took me to one side. "Stella, I'm going to beat them all. I'm going to win," she said. It wasn't even a question. "Sure you are, Mandy. You're the best," I said. And although I meant it, not just that she was the best cook, but that she was The Best, my best friend, it came out sounding pretty lame even to me.

But now as the silver van approached the shining steel gates of AgroGlobal headquarters, I wondered if she had meant something else altogether. A security guard scanned our ID chips and the gates slid open. The van drove up to the main gate, and my guys, the suits, got out with me. They walked me to the entrance, one on either side. A gray-haired man was waiting for us. He introduced himself as Professor Gulati, head of nutritional research, and shook my hand gravely. "Thank you for coming," he said politely, like I had any choice. "We need your help."

"Sure," I said. "What's this?"

"It's Mandira. She's a friend of yours, I believe. The thing is"—he coughed slightly—"she's disappeared."

I felt like my brain had just fused.

"What do you mean? That's not possible, is it? I mean, isn't that supposed to be impossible? You mean . . . you've lost my friend?"

"Calm down, Miss Jordan."

"I AM CALM!" I shouted. What about the tracker—the implants they put in all the contestants before they entered the Portal? What about the safeguards and rules and scanning and regulations? There had been a ton of them, all ratified by international treaty. Nothing was allowed into or out of the Portal except the contestants. They were stripped and scanned before each episode. We'd had it drummed into our heads forever: messing with time was a serious business, and nothing, *nothing* could be allowed to destabilize the Chronologic. One little mistake and our whole present could disappear, *vhooop*, up its own wormhole.

I was too busy freaking out to notice my surroundings, barely registering the long, gleaming corridors and glass archways. Professor Gulati finally stopped at a door and held it open for me. "We'd like you to take a look at the footage," he said. "Maybe you can spot something we've missed. You knew Mandira . . ."

I seriously didn't like the way he was talking about her in the past tense.

"We think she may have been planning this."

"She wouldn't!" But as I yelled, a vivid picture flashed in my mind of Mandy, that stubborn, crazy look she had in her eyes and I knew: she would. She totally would. *Mandy, you idiot, what have you done?* I groaned inwardly. *You are in an insane amount of trouble.*

Inside the screening room, there were five or six other men and women already sitting around, waiting for me, it seemed. There were desks and a large screen. Professor Gulati ushered me into a chair, and then turned to a guy wearing headphones sitting at one of the consoles. "Roll the film," he said, and then, as the lights went down he leaned across to me. "Rural Punjab, 2014," he whispered. "All this is unedited footage. Shot this morning."

Jerome looked a bit awkward in his long shirt, and he kept tripping on his baggy trousers, but Mandy looked really good on screen. She and Sherna were wearing long tunics and loose trousers gathered in folds around the ankles. Mandy's top had little spangly mirrors and embroidery on it. It was really colorful against her cocoa-colored skin and she looked—well, I have to admit that skinny old 2D looked quite beautiful as she stood there listening to Judge Kumar explain the challenge. "Makki ki roti and sarson ka saag lunch for fourteen. Forty-five minutes to prep, cook, and plate up," he said. The presentation was what Judge Dingle called "fast an' dirty," but it still had to be spot on: the steel plates shiny, the tumblers filled to the brim with frothy jeera-spiced lassi, and the ghee had to be made from scratch. It was tough, but it was supposed to be.

Each contestant was at their cook station in a different section of the screen, shot at different camera angles. The clock was ticking, and my heart seemed to beat a shade faster as I noticed that Sherna was falling behind. Jerome was already dry-roasting spices to season his sarson ka saag, which lay in the bowl in a smooth, bottle-green swirl. Mandy was rolling a wooden spindle expertly between the palms of her hands to whip the curd for frothy lassi, but Sherna was still struggling to get the right consistency for her roti dough. I heard one of the judges mumbling off-screen, then out loud: "You might want to add a bit more flour, love. Thirteen minutes to plate." She looked up, smearing one hand across her forehead and streaking her hair with dough.

"C'mon, c'mon," I found myself muttering under my breath. Of course I wanted Mandy to win, but—well, it was impossible not to want them *all* to make it. I glanced back to Mandy's corner of the screen—and it was empty.

There was a lot of commotion on-screen, people shouting and running, the camera careening around all over the place. And then the screen went blank.

When the lights came on, Professor Gulati turned to me. "Well, did you see anything? Anything at all? Something we might have missed?"

"I . . . I don't understand." I shook my head. "She can't have just disappeared . . . what about the tracker?"

"We . . . ah . . . found the tracker . . ."

I winced.

". . . but no sign of Mandira." Professor Gulati stood up. "What about before she left? Did she say anything to you? Did you notice anything different in her behavior?"

I shrugged. "No."

"Miss Jordan, you do realize the seriousness of what has happened? The Chronologic may have been compromised. We no longer know what might happen."

"Well, surely if something *had* happened, then, well— I mean, shouldn't we already know about it by now? Everything feels about the same to me. You're still here. I'm still here."

They asked me all kinds of questions about Mandy, and I answered them all. Well, most of them anyway. But all I really wanted to do was to get home, get back to somewhere dark and quiet where I could think.

It was late at night when they finally dropped me back. Marra and the others were really relieved to see me, but I just couldn't face any more questions. I had a Newtri and then slumped off to bed. I lay there for hours, it seemed like, until the house was still and silent. Then I crept downstairs and opened the door to the basement. I moved the crates and reached behind the pipe. I pulled out the toolbox and opened it. Right on top lay a piece of paper. I unfolded it carefully and smoothed it out.

Dearest Stella,

I guess by now you know I've gone off-grid. I don't know if you'll ever forgive me, but I owe you an explanation. It's the least I can do. When I go to MasterChef today, I'm not coming back. I've decided I can't live like this anymore. You remember in school they taught us all about the Dying Out? Years before it happened, this guy called Einstein said that if the bees disappeared, mankind would only last another four years. Well, he was wrong about that. Maybe we would have died out if it hadn't been for Newtri, but we're still here—you're still here. I know all about the Chronologic, I know it can't be changed, but I asked myself why? Why can't we change history? I've been in the past, Stella, I've eaten fresh strawberries, I've bitten apples, I've tasted freshly baked bread with a hunk of creamy brie, I've licked tandoori chicken masala off my fingers and drunk peppermint sherbet.

Maybe I can't change anything—but I know I've got to try. Perhaps if people know what life will be like without the bees, they'll be able to do something about it. I don't know. All I do know is that I want to live my life—and if I can't cook real food, I might survive, but I think I'll die.

Look after yourself my darling Stella-bella. And know that I will always be

Your best friend forever,

Mandy xxx

I couldn't believe I would never see her again. That my friend—who I saw *this morning*—was not just dead, but that she must have died a hundred years ago. I tried to cry, but the tears wouldn't come. Instead, I found myself filled with this strange, insane, bubbling, uplifting feeling. The Chronologic was broken. Or if not broken, then at least cracked. And through that little crack, the light came in. Fragging hell, Mandy, what on earth have you started? And then I started to laugh. Because I knew that even though everything was exactly the same, nothing ever would be, ever again.

The men who had raised these walls around her had looked into her eyes with such pity. Surely one of them would have left a gap?

But no, not even a hundredth of an inch.

They would not risk the displeasure of the Emperor, ruler of Hindustan, the man who has had Anarkali entombed alive.

A slave girl married to the Prince? NEVER!

She takes a deep breath and presses her palms against the stone.

It is the coolest time of night. Winter fog swirls around the fortress.

If only Prince Salim would come and rescue her.

Is he under arrest?

Is he drugged?

There is no room for her to bend her knees or hang her head. All she can do is stare at these blocks of stone.

She imagines the Emperor of the World looking down into the valley...

... at the distant fields, the shimmering river, the dots of color that are the farmer women's odhnis.

She remembers how rich she felt in her simple odhni, each time the Prince looked at her. He had promised her a hundred new dresses if she let the hem of her skirt graze his cheek.

Salim.

She had willingly traded her life to save the rebel Prince.

Concentric circles of gray ice press against the back of her eyelids. She pushes her fingers into the stone. Warm. Cold. Her skin. Her nails. Her blood. Her toes, the only part of her that touches soft earth instead of hard stone.

Stop! Stop mocking me.

TRY

Even if she could smash her way out, how would she get past the guards?

They will catch me again.

Anarkali's fingers are cold; she can no longer tell the difference between her skin and the stone.

One step at a time. Once you tackle this wall, all walls will yield.

Am I going mad?

A white heat rises under her feet and travels up into her body and head. Every nerve jangles. It is as if she has been struck by lightning. Rivers crawl under her muscles. Streams press out of her nostrils. Her eyes are a furnace.

Everything that comes from me is me.

Stone is me.

Fire is me. Water is me. You are me. And if you will it, I can be you.

She can see nothing but the pinkish-yellow sandstone. It grates against her eyeballs.

Now what?

Where did you go?

Tell me what to do.

She finds that she can turn her head. Can her arms move too? What about her feet?

YES

It is harder walking through stone but she knows she can escape. But first she needs food and water. And Salim.

The Prince must be told.

Now there is a real chance for both of them. They could go somewhere else, far from palace intrigue and battles. Not even the Emperor of the World could stop them.

She moves within the wall to the Queen Mother's entertaining room. It will be empty at this hour but she can find bowls of dried fruit and sherbet.

She presses her body against the wall. With a jerk and a stumble she falls into the room

She eats slowly. One almond, one raisin, one date, then more sherbet. She knows that those who have been hungry too long must not eat too quickly.

When she hears footsteps, she steps back into the wall.

This time it's easier. Her eyes no longer burn.

She makes her way to the men's quarters in the royal apartments.

The last time she was here, she'd been summoned for the Emperor's evening entertainment.

This is where Salim had fallen in love with her.

As she surges toward the sheesh mahal, a place that had been so enchanting once, she is able to see through the walls. She wonders why this room and not others?

She opens and shuts her eyes a few times and realizes that she can see through thousands of tiny mirrors embedded in the stone.

But now she must leave the security of walls. A garden lies between the palace and the Prince's chamber.

Crouching low, she wonders if she can walk right under the guard's feet.

It is all earth, stone, mud and water.

She presses herself up against the floor of Salim's bedchamber.

She can feel his presence.

Is his spirit broken? Is he wounded?

She remembers how hard he fought when the soldiers came to arrest her.

Anarkali.

She explains that she has found a way out of the fortress. But there is no time to waste.

Where are we going?

Somewhere else. ANYWHERE.

And do what? I am Prince of Hindustan! A future Emperor of the World!

And what am I?

You are my beloved Anarkali, still alive! If only you knew how much I have missed you.

Missed me? Is that all you can say?

Anarkali looks hard at him. She has not walked through walls for nothing. The Prince must come away with her.

LET'S GO.

Be reasonable, my love. We can't get past a whole army.

She has always done as he wished. But now she must take the lead. And he must follow.

Trust me. We can.

Where? Anarkali! What...

Just push

Salim resists. But this is no time for gentle persuasion. She digs in her heels and pulls with every last shred of her power.

And then it happens. They are through.

Keep breathing.

URGGGHH!

Stone breathes too, you know.

She turns her attention to urgent matters. She needs water.

I feel I'm burning up inside.

They have a long walk ahead and the going will be very slow.

She leads Salim by the hand. They move south, further and further into the heart of the earth until they touch water.

The alarm will be raised. The fortress gates will be sealed. The cavalry will be dispatched.

But they will not know where to look. She will find valleys, rivers, forests full of fruit and meat. It will be a long time before Salim can walk through walls himself...

She will teach him to listen to the whispering of the earth. And when he does he will see how easy it is to walk away from palaces, and never look back.

Cast Out

Samhita Arni

I was eight years old when I discovered what happened to the girls who tried to do magic. It was the day they brought Dewi to the beach. She was the most beautiful girl in our village, but on that day her head was shaved and she was dressed in sackcloth. Her face was streaked with tears. There were deep scratches on either cheek, and her arms were badly bruised. The blacksmith pulled her by steel chains wrapped around her wrists toward the boat by the water.

It wasn't really a boat. Just a barrel, sawed in half.

The blacksmith pushed her onto her knees, and the headman stepped forward, carrying a whip.

Before us, they flogged her. I winced with every lash. But

Dewi never cried out. I could see her bite her lip, the sweat gather on her brow. As blood began to bead and stain her sackcloth shift, Dewi's mother, standing right in front of me, screamed.

It felt like it went on for hours, lash after lash. I turned my face away, burrowing into my mother's dress, but she grabbed my chin and forced my head forward, to keep me watching.

Lash after lash.

Later, I found out what had happened. Dewi and her sister, Indah, had been out in the forest, gathering wood, when they had been surprised by brigands—fierce, desperate men who haunted our forests and preyed on travelers.

The men had surrounded the two girls, and held them down. They had broken Indah's wrist as she struggled to break free, and had kicked Dewi in the ribs.

Dewi, scared and angry, did the unthinkable.

The thing that we're all taught never to do. The thing that we know if we ever show a sign of, we'll be killed.

She set them on fire with her magic.

Dewi confessed, after twelve lashes. She'd had the magic for years. Then the blacksmith pushed her into the barrel, and set her out to sea.

Far off on the horizon, a Demon Cloud glimmered.

We watched her drift, borne by the ocean, toward the cloud.

Every child knows that the world is round, and there are two vast continents separated by an ocean that girdles the world. North is a land shaped like the wings of an eagle and studded with mountains. South is a continent formed like a flower and filled with green forests.

Once, there was a third land, East, a continent of beautiful lakes and shining cities with spires that pierced the sky. The kings of North and South envied the king of East, and together waged war on him. They ordered their sorcerers to build a mighty weapon with the power of a thousand suns. This weapon turned the shining cities of East to ash. Mountains toppled, the earth quaked and split, and the ocean rose up to claim the land. The people of East, dying, cursed their foes in North and South.

That curse took shape and form, turning into the black Demon Clouds that scour the skies above the ocean and hound our ships to this day as they sail between North and South.

Some tales speak of clouds that unleash a rain of fire. Others tell of clouds that expel poisonous fumes. There are even more sinister tales—of shrieking faces glimpsed in the clouds, of demons who descend to eat the sailors, and send their bones, picked clean, back to the shore. But still ships set sail, for the rewards are plentiful: spices from South are much in demand here in North, while our silk commands exorbitant prices in South. Ships that attempt the crossing must carry onboard a pair of powerful sorcerers, who can keep away the clouds and ward the ship's course.

Once there were many magicians in North and South, but now there are few. Any boy who shows the slightest sign of magical ability is taken immediately to the king's stronghold, where he is trained by the king's magicians to guide and protect our ships.

But no girl can be a magician. If it is discovered that we can wield magic, we suffer a sentence worse than death.

We are set on the ocean, hands and legs bound, hair cut off, and our magic stunned by a special brew of herbs. An untrained magician is no match for the clouds. Even if Dewi could have bested the Demon Clouds, she would still succumb to thirst and hunger, adrift on the vast ocean.

Can you imagine a more miserable death?

A few months after Dewi's fatal incident, my mother went into labor and delivered a baby girl. And late one moonless night when my sister was only a few weeks old, I woke up to find that my mother had disappeared and the cradle was empty.

I crept out of the house, and saw my mother, carrying my sister, headed toward the beach. I followed her. The baby squalled as the wind broke across the waves. I remember that my mother was tired and wan after her lying-in, and she walked slowly across the sand. She carried my sister in a small basket made of reeds.

When my mother reached the shore, she knelt by the water's edge and placed the basket on the waves.

And she watched my sister disappear into the night.

I have asked myself many times why I didn't say something. Why I didn't scream, why I didn't shout out. Would that have stopped my mother? If she knew I was watching?

I didn't say anything. I knew that it was because my sister was a girl, and my parents had hoped for a boy. For the people of my village, the birth of a daughter was a curse. Girls were expensive, a burden, not something one wished for.

I thought of my little sister and Dewi each time I went to the shore, and saw the ocean vomit bones onto the beach. Small, fragile bones, picked clean. The bones of birds or fish. Or of something else.

It was my mother who discovered that I had magic, a few months after my eleventh birthday, the same month my menses began.

It was the night of a storm. A peal of thunder had woken her, to find me missing from my pallet. Frightened, she had ventured into the storm to find me in the pasture beyond our cottage.

I was suspended in midair. Above me, lightning raced across the sky. Clouds clashed and roared. The rain didn't touch me. Somehow, impossibly, the drops had coalesced into a shining sphere of water that enshrouded me.

My mother was terrified. "Karthini!" she shrieked. Above the din of the storm and the pounding rain, somehow, I awoke. For an all-too-brief moment I saw the skies flash above me, saw the shining nimbus of raindrops around me. Then the skies scattered, the ground rose up to meet me, and the sphere of water broke over me.

"Karthini, you must control it," my mother told me later, as I sat shivering and wet after she had hustled me inside. When I didn't answer, she shook me savagely. I turned and saw tears running fast down her face. "Promise me!"

But I recalled the intoxicating feeling of being up there, in midair. The sense of time slowing. A tingle in my fingers and toes, a beat in my blood, a warm shiver up my spine. The eerie beauty of flashing skies, and the exhilaration of being dry in the midst of a storm.

"Why can't girls do magic?" I asked. "Why not?"

"They just can't." My mother gripped me fiercely, so tightly that it hurt. "Promise me, Karthini—I beg you—that you won't try."

I had promised. I could control the magic during the day but nights were another matter. I would dream of riding the moon, flying in the expanse between the stars, and would wake to find myself drifting toward the roof of our small cottage.

So my mother brewed me a special tea that made my dreams dark. A recipe, passed down through generations, that her mother had taught her, to bring about a slumber so thick and heavy that I could no longer succumb to the lure of magic in my sleep.

But it meant I had no dreams.

Three years later my father disappeared. The harvest had been a poor one and had forced him to turn to fishing. The day he went missing, he had glanced at the sky, as usual, before setting sail. It was clear. Not a cloud on the horizon. But an hour later, the Demon Clouds had gathered, mustering close, spitting fire.

He never returned.

A few days later, the ocean spewed up a bolus of bone and wood and sail upon our beach. My mother took ill immediately. Within months she faded and died, and I was left an orphan.

And so I went to live with my uncle and aunt, and earned my keep by watching their two youngest boys, Sigid and Musa, eight and ten years old.

One morning, not long afterward, I took my cousins with me to gather the snake fruit from the plants that grew by our cliffs. The youngest, Sigid, pranced around with a toy sword.

"I'm going to be a soldier!" he exclaimed, and waved his wooden sword in the air.

I told him to be careful, but he shook his head at me and continued with his play. He slammed his sword onto the branches of a dragon plant, and a hummingbird darted out and pecked at his face.

Startled, Sigid stumbled backward, onto the edge of the cliff—

And into thin air.

Musa screamed.

What happened next was so fast, it's all a blur in my memory. One moment, Sigid was tumbling past the cliffs to the rocks beneath, and the next he was lying on the ground before me, quivering with terror. Musa stared at me with fear and revulsion.

I had used magic to pull Sigid to safety.

And so my turn came too, by the beach.

* * *

I wasn't brave like Dewi. I wept and begged for my life. I pleaded with my aunt and uncle to spare me—after all, hadn't I saved their son? My aunt wept too, and turned her face away, but my uncle was implacable.

Like Dewi, I was dressed in a sackcloth shift. The blacksmith wrapped steel chains around my wrist and dragged me, crying, across the beach. When I tried to pull back, he tugged, and I tripped, tumbling over the sand, to come to rest sprawled by the water's edge.

The headman was waiting there, his whip coiled around one fist. The first two lashes bit into my flesh. I screamed. The third lash drew blood. With the next lash my back was a writhing, red-hot mass of pain.

I broke down. I told them everything they wanted to hear.

They thrust me, as they had thrust Dewi, into a sawed-off barrel that bobbed on the water.

But as they pushed the barrel out to sea, a woman cried out "Wait!"

She ran to me. I knew who she was—Satyawati. She already had five children, and the little baby she held in her arms was her sixth, a girl born a few months after her husband died.

She pushed the baby at me.

I shook my head.

"Please, please take her," she cried. "Look after her."

"No . . . I can't—"

Satyawati sobbed, "Just take her. Please."

I tried to turn away, but my hands were bound. Satyawati leaned over and placed the baby in my lap.

"Her name is Sari," she whispered to me.

I thought, as we drifted on the ocean, that Satyawati was mad. Why had she given her daughter to me?

Black clouds clustered close to the horizon. Even if clouds didn't kill us, hunger and thirst would soon enough. How long could a baby survive without food?

How long would I?

Soon the Demon Clouds came.

My heart started to race. I could feel sweat gather in my armpits, on my palms, down my bleeding, burning back. With an effort, I pushed the pain away and thought about what I had to do.

The stories I had heard described demons living in the clouds. Demons with razor-sharp teeth, and forked tongues, with a hundred terrible blood-red eyes and faces from your most terrible nightmares.

But this was different. There were no faces, no shrieking, laughing demons—just an unending bank of black clouds, menacing and spanning the sky as far as you could see.

I will never forget that night, as long as I live. Green fumes emerged from the clouds. Sari started to cough, and I felt something scratch at the back of my throat.

And then a drop of fire fell from the sky and touched my hand.

It was as though a thousand pieces of glass had smashed through my skin. I screamed out in pain, and the baby began to cry.

I can't explain what I did at that moment—but it was magic. You'll never understand it until you do it yourself.

I don't know where it came from—but I think when your life is in danger, the mind has a strange way of knowing what will help you to survive. It was as if, in the moment before, my mind had been an octopus. I had felt fear, worry, hunger, thirst, pain, a desire to protect Sari, grief—these were the many tentacles of my mind, the many things jostling for my attention.

And then there was a tingle in my fingers and toes, a warm shiver that raced down my spine, and my mind changed shape. From a many-tentacled beast, it turned into a smooth, pure muscle. This muscle consumed everything else—every thought, worry, and fear—and turned it into a shield, hard as a diamond.

The rain of fire slid over it, harmlessly, and dripped into the sea.

The edges of our barrel burned and smoked. As the fire struck the sea, it lit the waters below. I could see schools of fish writhing in the water where the scorching rain fell. Green ribbons of flame twisted through the ocean. The carcass of a bird, charred to a cinder, plunged beneath the surface.

The shield gave me hope and strength. I found the will to twist my hands free. The chains cut and gouged and bloodied my wrists until finally they slipped off. I held Sari tight, in my bleeding hands, while I used everything I had to keep up the invisible shield between us and the Demon Clouds.

But that wasn't all. As the fire-rain beat on, the ocean rose up to meet the sky. The waves tossed our tiny barrel back and forth, and sheets of water drenched us, again and again, through the night.

I struggled to shelter Sari from both fire and water. I don't know how long it went on for. It was the longest night of my life, and each minute felt like an hour, each hour like a day. But finally we passed the Demon Clouds. And beyond the clouds, the sky was starting to turn from blue to pink. Dawn was breaking.

It was then that I spotted the ship—a black ship, with black sails, quite unlike any other I had seen before.

I was too weak to raise my hand and signal to it. My voice died in my parched throat. I was scared that the ship would pass us by. Desperate, I tried something that I had only imagined until then.

I screamed at the ship with my mind.

A few minutes later, the vessel turned toward us. Soon enough, it was just a few feet away. A ladder descended, and a sailor climbed down.

I watched him, wary despite my relief. How would these people treat us? Would they, like the headman and blacksmith of my village, flog and sentence girls to death for practicing magic? Would they take in Sari, or would they cast her out to sea, the way my mother had my sister? Would they despise Sari and me for being girls? Or— though I could not imagine it—would girls here meet even worse fates?

When the sailor reached the bottom of the ladder, he swung around to jump into our barrel. He was a strange-looking man—smaller and more slender than the men at home. I thought that he must be a man from South— perhaps they looked different from us, just as men from our village look different from men from the mountains.

But as he took Sari from my hands to pass her to another man behind him on the ladder, I noticed something strange.

This sailor wasn't a man. This sailor was a woman.

The ship was called the *Pearl*. Later, I learned that there are many such ships on the ocean, sailing between North and South. All these ships have black sails and their crews are made up of women so powerful in magic that no Demon Cloud can stop them. And every few months, each ship returns to Floating Island—an isle in the middle of the ocean.

This was where the *Pearl* was headed when they found me. As the sailors said, a ship is no place to raise a child— and there were many women on Floating Island who would care for and raise Sari.

How do I describe Floating Island? It is beautiful, with a natural harbor and beaches of white sand. You would never have heard of Floating Island. It's not on any map that has been made in North or South, and it has never been discovered by a ship crewed by men.

There is a town by the harbor—we call it Shiptown. There are many women here, of all ages. Some fix the ships, others farm fields, while others weave cloth and make goods that our ships trade with smugglers on the coasts of North and South.

Of course, we make things with magic. We have for years, but it is only recently I realized that our magic and these objects could serve another purpose. It came to me one day as I worked on a piece of cloth, woven with magic to shimmer at night. Sari, who at eight years old was eternally curious, watched me work and asked, "Karthini, what are you weaving?"

I told her that I was making a piece of cloth that sailors on board ships like the *Pearl* would trade with smugglers, who would in turn sell it to merchants in the cities. Such a cloth would fetch a great price for a rich merchant's or nobleman's daughter. And that is how the cloth that I made might one day be worn by a bride on her wedding day.

"Like Teacher Suki?"

I paused. Suki was Sari's teacher, who had come to the island a few years ago. A wealthy trader's daughter from South, Suki had been on her way to an arranged marriage with her father's trading partner in North. Her fiancé was two decades older and had already buried three wives. Suki had set sail in one of her father's vessels. Desperate to avoid the marriage, she had escaped en route in one of the ship's small boats and had been picked up a few days later by one of our ships.

I nodded. "Suki would have worn something like this had she got married."

Sari frowned. "But suppose the girl who wears this wants to run away, like Suki, on the night of her wedding?"

I didn't have an answer.

"Couldn't she come here?"

"But how would she find this place?" I countered.

And Sari came up with a surprising answer, an answer that stunned me with its simplicity. "Why can't we tell her?" She fingered the shimmering pattern on the cloth. "Can't you use your magic to weave a story, like this design, into the cloth?"

And so we began to use magic to weave stories and maps into the things we made, just as, in the past, we had used magic to create tiles that constantly changed color, a carpet with a sheen like moonlight, or lace with a shimmering pattern. It is one of these things you hold in your hands— it might be a piece of cloth, a pattern on a tile, or the embroidery on a wedding veil.

Our magic also works to protect the secret of Floating Island. Only if you are alone, and a woman or a girl, will the story reveal itself to you. If you dream of a different life or if you are in danger—snip off a piece of this cloth, tease out a thread of this carpet, or break off a piece of this tile, and carry it with you.

Come to the coast and watch the horizon for a ship with black sails. Be sure that the piece of cloth or thread is with you. When you spot such a ship, wait for when the tide is low. If you can, steal a boat or build a makeshift raft, or—if you are a strong swimmer—swim toward the ship.

Once the piece of cloth or thread that you carry with you touches water, it will send out a signal that only we will hear. And we will come for you.

Weft

Alyssa Brugman

Beauty hurts. Don't let anyone tell you different. Hair is usually not so bad. It's the paying part that kills. I was laid out for weeks. My back still hurts from the surgery. I have phantom kidney pain, they tell me. I wonder who has my kidney now? It's a man, probably, with high blood pressure and diabetes. Maybe my absent kidney hurts me every time he considers eating a cheeseburger?

I'm glad it's done, though. I'll spend my credit on ludicrously robust, tousled bed-hair, and then Botox, so I never have to look like I've had a deep, face-contorting thought. Maybe a tiny brow-lift somewhere in my thirties. Totally new boobs when I turn forty. Not bigger, just back where they were. Laser my rear-end every twelve months after that. Eventually I'll have to forfeit a cornea to keep that up.

Have you ever noticed that celebrities have universally good hair? Even when the paparazzi catch them on the street with no makeup on, buying takeout cappuccinos and they are looking all hunted and irritated and fraught? It might be stuffed under a baseball cap, and scruffy, but it's still long and thick, and not endsy. Of course, they have proper money to spend on it. They don't have to apply for credit the way that we normal people do. But still . . .

My hair is endsy and thin. When it's clean it has a speed hump in the middle, as if I have been wearing it in a ponytail. And my bed-hair isn't tousled and sexy. It clings to my neck, seaweed style, as though I'm recovering from a near-drowning incident.

I know you're thinking, *It's just hair.* But hair is a big deal. Being a person with shocking hair, I've spent quite a long time pondering it, and I have a theory.

Here's what I think—attractiveness in most species has to do with whether you're going to be a good breeder, right? So when a guy looks at an hourglass-shaped girl, the caveman part of his brain is going, *My, those broad hips will readily pass a giant infant cranium. Those hefty bosoms will provide abundant sustenance to my sons! I will mate with her!*

And hair is a sign that you're a good breeder too. When hair is glossy and thick and long, it's like a record growing out of your head of how healthy you have been over the last few years. It's a big flag saying that you've got robust immune function. Or, on the other hand, your crap hair says that you're sickly and weak, and while you might pop out a little feeble one, you're going to be a burden.

I'm not talking about the big sensible part of your brain that says, *No, no, I seek a partner who is my intellectual equal, who will share proportionally in the housework.* I'm as guilty as the next human of clocking a colossal set of latissimus dorsi and thinking, just in that first millisecond, in the cavegirl part of my brain, *Drool, those lats are going to catch and carry home a substantial beast that will provide plenteous protein during my child-bearing. I will make him aware of the broadness of my pelvis right this minute.* I mean, who doesn't? Those people are liars! Or they just are not in touch with their cavepeople brains.

How is it, then, that celebrities have universally long, glossy hair when, as a sample population, they have a higher than average chance of having an (insert illegal substance here) habit? Addictions are not generally consistent with bristling good health.

I have found out the secret. They wear another lady's hair. Yes, that's right!

Anyone can do it, if you have money or credit. Every normal person has to apply for credit eventually, if you want to look any good. So I applied. I decided on a kidney, because I've got another one, right? They were able to book in my nephrectomy straight away, but the booking at the salon took ages.

Finally I'm in the specialist salon. They do weaves, braids or dreads, injectables and fillers too, while you wait.

My stylist is called Casey. She could be eighteen or thirty-five. I can't tell, because she has that mineral makeup matte thing going on. I love the way that looks, but it's hard to get the measure of a person that way. I have always wondered if the craggy, crinkly contours our faces make when we think deeply about things make the real shape that we are. If we ever allowed ourselves to get old, our faces would be a montage of all the most intense thoughts we had. What would that look like?

But we don't do that. Why would we, when we can iron it all out, stretch the skin across our bones like canvas over a frame? Then we find a graphic that matches who we think we would like to be, and we ink that on our hide.

Casey has a frangipani on the inside of her wrist. She's summer, and sweetness.

The girl in the chair across the room has *faith* on the back of her neck.

Faith.

Like, *all* faith? Pfft!

If I use some of my credit for a tattoo, I would want it to be words. Something I believe. Something I don't want to forget, and something that makes me glow up from the inside every time I look at it, but I'm not sure what I believe that much yet.

Maybe I should choose *doubt?* That's unlikely to escape me at any point, is it?

There are a hundred words that are more specific than *faith.* Fidelity. Constance. Promise. Courage. Zeal.

How can you sum up what you want everyone else to know about you in one word?

Faith? What does that mean? Unless her name is Faith and she has a short-term memory thing, in which case she should have put it on her forehead, or on the back of her hand.

Why has she put a tattoo where she can't see it?

Do you know what I should get tattooed on my neck? "Apathy is like . . . whatever." But would it be funny *forever*? No. Because it doesn't define me. In some respects I'm quite driven. Determined enough to have a nephrectomy for credit.

I catch the tattoo girl's eye in the mirror.

"Why have you got *faith* written on the back of your neck?"

She starts to answer, but the stylist next to me turns on the blow-dryer, and I can see her mouth moving, but I don't know what she's saying, so I just nod until she stops, and then check my phone for messages. There are none, but I squint intently and flick and tap as if I am superpopular, and a little put out by the amount of correspondence I have to attend to during my me-time.

Casey hands me the weft. She's letting me hold it while she starts the plait that will hold it in place on my head. It's probably about seventy centimeters long. It's thicker than mine—strong and shiny.

I ask Casey where it comes from.

"Poor people," she says.

"Why?" I ask.

"It has to be virgin hair," Casey explains. "Not hair from virgins—hair that hasn't been colored or permed before. Rich people don't have virgin hair."

I picture my hair donor to be about seventeen. There's a toddler squatting on the floor, engrossed in some game, and a baby on her lap. She's in a hut. She's brushing her beautiful waist-length hair, and then she painstakingly plucks each strand out of the brush. With her callused hands she weaves the strands one at a time into the cotton thread that will bind them before sale. She ties the rest of her hair into a knot on her head, and then she carries her babies out into the fields to pick vegetables. From a distance, the wealthy farmer who employs her measures the width of her hips with a calculating eye.

"Sometimes they cut off their hair in a religious ceremony to show their devotion."

Now I see an altar. And the girls lined up, on their knees, heads bowed, their beautiful long hair brushing against their shoulder blades. There's a priest holding some kind of ceremonial shears. All the hair goes into a basket, ready to be sanitized and have the color stripped from it.

But at least it's not a kidney, right? I mean, hair will grow back.

I rub my finger along the braid. It's tight and feels like a scar.

"Do they know where it goes?" I ask.

Casey doesn't answer.

While Casey works, I look across the hallway where some ladies are using their credit for manicures. As if you would waste it on that! Nails I can do myself.

Casey reaches forward, takes my weft, and I give it up

reluctantly. She must have been a good prospect, my hair donor. She's called Anala, or Ananya, or Anushka. It's an A name anyway.

Casey's weaving Ananya's hair into my hair. She's using a needle and thread, binding me to her. Then she's finished and she's off to the little secret back room where they make up the colors.

Is it lying, having Ananya's hair entwined with mine? Is it wrong to fool someone else's caveman brain? Does my seaweed straggle tell the world that I am a burden, and is it true?

You know the weird thing? We put on our faces each day, that make our eyes look bigger, and our lips juicier, and it's all lies, but then we get mad when Mr. Colossal-Latissimus-Dorsi doesn't love us for who we are. Or even Mr. Borrowed-Kidney-Cheeseburger-Eater.

But have you ever tried not doing it? Have you ever gone out in track pants, with no hair and makeup? You go invisible. Eyes just slide over you as if you were never there. You could totally commit felonies. You could line up at the checkout of a supermarket on Christmas Eve, hold up the place, and make your getaway on a motorized scooter you have stolen from an octogenarian on the way out. Still no one would pick you in a lineup. It's the bits we add to ourselves that make us memorable.

I know there are some naturally beautiful people, but I mean in real life. When was the last time you saw a genuinely striking unaugmented individual, in person, in your neighborhood, during the day? Were you drunk?

I'm not talking about people who are naturally beautiful as a package of attributes. There are heaps of those. I'm not talking about little kids either. I mean a grown person who stirs your caveperson from twenty meters away, when you are sober, and before you know that they are generous, or funny, or artistic—someone who is not spending their credit being waxed, collagened, and lasered, and lunge-walking backward to the organic market to buy quinoa, coconut water, and goji berries.

They are mythical creatures. They are Bigfoots. You've never come across a Bigfoot? This is my point.

But if you ever did see a Bigfoot, you'd go all cray-cray and gobsmacked, and extreme, like you'd been just a tiny bit tasered.

Do you think that's why the celebrities look hunted and irritated and fraught when they get caught in the wild? Because there is a very high chance that any second they are going to be accosted by some caveperson who's going to scream, and wet their pants, and thrash around, and maybe assault them? I would probably take cocaine and have all of the panic syringed off my face too, under those circumstances.

Real beauty is rare. It kind of runs the world, and we want it. We could go mad trying to make it happen. People do, and not just women.

I stroke Ananya's hair. It's stupendously long. It looks great already. It brushes against the small of my back. Faith smiles at me in the mirror. I think of asking her again about her tattoo, but I just don't care that much.

I think about asking her what she gave for credit, but we don't talk about that. Not in here.

Casey comes back and starts painting my scalp with the cold, thick purple chemicals that will make me and my weft the same color. Dab, dab, dab. It has that funny astringent ammonia smell. Not virgin hair anymore. Slutty, colored hair now.

Casey rinses off my hair with scalding water in long strokes. She rubs at the binding scar. She dries my hair. It takes a long time, because Ananya's hair is so thick and healthy and hydrated. Then she burns it into long, uncontrived ringlets. I'm tousled in a non-drowned way. It looks hotter than I had imagined. Even my own cavegirl brain is impressed.

She swipes my credit card casually, as though she doesn't know how I earned it, and I'm wondering if the woman being exploited here is me.

Then Ananya's hair and I flounce past the nail place. Flounce, flounce. I catch my reflection in a shop that sells soaps, candles, and hand lotions. Who's that woman with the great hair? Wait, that's us! I give my hair a tug. It's very secure. I hope Ananya got paid. I hope she has access to goji berries and coconut water, so her hair grows fast and she doesn't have to marry the farmer.

But then, it's just hair, right? It's not a kidney.

the Wednesday Room

Written by Kushali Manickavel
Drawn by Lily Mae Martin
2013.

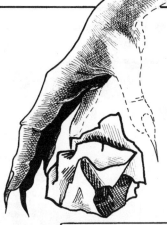

Come on. Let's try again.

Forget it. Doesn't matter anyway.

But standardizing means you'll finally fit in. Isn't that what you've always wanted?

Munro has her final standardization appraisal tomorrow. She says that if she gets rejected she's going to ride her bicycle straight into the tar canals and kill herself.

Do you think I should ride into the tar canals if they reject me too?

Why? So you can smell like hot vomit when you are dead?

Come on, read it again.

Read the part about your family.

STATE-SPONSORED COMPLETE AND IRREVERSIBLE STANDARDIZATION REQUEST—

EXPLAIN WHY YOU SHOULD BE CHOSEN FOR THIS PROCEDURE, PAYING SPECIAL ATTENTION TO YOUR FAMILY HISTORY AND THE EFFECT YOUR STANDARDIZATION WILL HAVE ON COMPLETE SOCIETAL STANDARDIZATION.

Oh God! My family is mostly a bunch of really weird women

They do things like collect drunk pixies that stop up people's toilets.

Getting pixies drunk was always fun!

Hey! Let's do that!

We can get some whiskey —

The pixies are gone, remember?

Oh right. Forgot.

Come on, read.

STANDARDIZATION
the hallmark of
VILIZATION

My name is Kavya...

I'm the last of the Cleaner Clan. We communicate with

supernatural beings. We weren't always Cleaners though—

They don't want to hear that.

But it's true!

Yeah, you're right.

Now we just contain supernatural

elements in society.

You were forced to.

They don't want to hear that either.

And no "Supernatural," it's "Substandard aberrations" or SAs, remember?

I am too fabulous to be an SA.

Hey, it's a joke.

I never thought of any of you that way.

Not even that senile unicorn who kept charging you?

unicorn mansion

She decorated her house so it would stay. Even if she couldn't...

Keep reading.

SAs cause annoyances like lost keys or temperamental toilets. Before standardization they had magical powers —

Yeah, yeah, they don't want to hear that ...

Keep the temperamental toilets, they'll like that.

SAs are invisible to everyone except us. We collect them in The Wednesday Room. It has landscapes, rooms, and is quite —

"Unique" sounds more standardized.

PFFT.

My aunt built the libraries, mountains...

Grandma built the pool table park, planted the cardtrees...

I would come and fight with the vampires, watch the mermaids play poker...

This is the one place I didn't feel ... substandard...

But I could never stay.

Guess I'm an SA freak.

"Freak" always makes me think of a tiny elephant...

...or Munro.

Keep reading.

Four months ago, I began partial standardization...

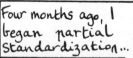

And I discovered that it makes SAs... disappear.

At first I thought they were just hiding.

But even when I went for collections, there were no SAs...

Other SAs in the facility noticed too.

Unicorns, Vampires. Pixies.

They   ...just...

...vanished.

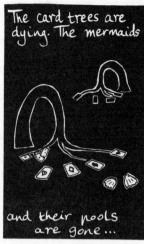

The card trees are dying. The mermaids

and their pools are gone...

Go on.

I'm applying for state-sponsored complete and irreversible standardization

because I believe it will make SAs and the facility permanently...

disappear.

End it with "this will be invaluable to societal standardization" blah, blah, blah...

Make sure you write something good. OK?

Yeah.

Do you think it hurts? When they disappear?

Nah. It's probably like falling asleep or something.

You're not scared? Of disappearing?

How about we go for a walk? The zombies might still be playing football.

Shouldn't we finish this first?

It'll still be here when we get back. It can wait.

Cool

Manjula Padmanabhan

Irfan leaned forward in his seat, waiting to sign in to his Home Languages class when . . .

Parp-parp-parp!

Lights flashing on his console!

Vibrations in the pod-frame!

He groaned. An emergency. Again.

"PodTwo," he said into the mouthpiece of his helmet, as he glanced up and confirmed the situation. "Incoming at twenty-oh-fifteen." Though the pods were pressurized, SpitRiders wore life-support on their heads at all times. Just in case. "Strapped in. Ready to go."

Being ready was fundamental to the space miner's life. Continuous, all-day alerts. No fallback if a SpitRider failed to respond to a signal. Serious consequences if performance statistics fell below minimum expectations.

Irfan's fifteen-year-old body was like a slender whip, all muscle and tension. Perfect for spending hours coiled into the ScholarPod, from which he could attend classes and do his lessons while monitoring his section of the station's boundary. He wore a skintight suit bristling with electronic aids. His honey-brown skin was smooth and hairless. The cap of tight curls on his head was always cropped short.

His tiny spherical vehicle shot out from its docking cradle like a bullet aimed at the star-spangled void of space. The interior of its transparent hull rippled with glowing numbers. Irfan spotted the faint orange dot that was his target. It wasn't visible to the naked eye. Even on the SmartGlass screen, it was only a blur at this distance.

"Irfan—?" That was Erdovan, the station captain. Irfan's father.

"I see it, Dad," said Irfan. He locked his sensors so that the object remained at the center of the screen. The pod's humming microjets fired in short bursts, repositioning the vehicle. Within seconds it was moving in a smooth curve toward the glowing chunk. "Locked on," he said into his mouthpiece. "Closing."

It wasn't really dangerous, what he and others like him did. It just took precision and full concentration. SpitRiders had to be small enough to fit inside the pods, they had to be at peak physical efficiency to respond instantly to alerts, and they had to be ferociously focused. Once they achieved their performance level, all they had to do was maintain it for four years. Exceeding the mark led to bonuses. And bonuses led all the way back to that distant, shining blue marble called Earth. The home that none of the young pod jockeys had ever known.

"I see it now," said Erdovan, who was monitoring the quadrant from his remote console. "Be careful. It's a spinner." Erdovan had been in the first teams to harvest the precious mineral known humorously as Flying Spit. Its official name was Saturnium: the molten lumps of matter thrown off by Saturn9, a small dark moon orbiting the ringed giant, Saturn. Saturn9 had only been identified after an exploratory MissionProbe parked itself in the planet's vicinity forty years ago.

The whole maneuver would be over in less than six minutes. For Irfan, however, that was beyond eternity. His Home Languages class had already begun. Yes, it lasted a full two hours. But the first half hour was the one that he lived and breathed for.

The orange blip on his screen had grown rapidly from the size of a sesame seed to grape pit to pistachio and in seconds would be at hazelnut.

"Closing," said Irfan. The sizes were precise definitions, named for food items that belonged to the distant home world. He could see the Spit's spin now, a trail of translucence extending behind the hazelnut. Good. That meant the pod was properly aligned alongside the trajectory of the speeding object, leaning in toward it.

Walnut. Prune.

"Steady, steady," said Erdovan in Irfan's ears. "It's wobbling. You might be too close—"

Plum. Peach.

I know, Dad, I know, thought Irfan. Out loud he said, "Forward thrusters trimmed." The blackness of space had become a crazy quilt of flashing zigzag lines now as the pod powered forward toward the object. The object had reached mango. The trail behind it looked like a dozen crystalline streamers, twirling in tight formation.

"Any moment now—" His father's voice was tense. Irfan could imagine Erdovan's face, the lean lines, the engraved creases in the skin. They were close, though Irfan had three brothers and two sisters. Irfan was the eldest.

There! Visual contact. A smooth object, shaped like a teardrop and eye-smartingly bright, was hurtling out to space two hundred meters from his position.

SNAP! He spanked down the twin bolt-generators with the open palms of both hands. A single hard punch of energy slammed directly onto the tail of the speeding object.

BLANG! The pod jarred back from the recoil.

Then *ZZZZZtrannggg!* It was a make-believe sound that Irfan heard only inside his head: the boom of the Spit being whacked on its tail, off its original course and at the precise angle that would send it directly into the station's receiving bay.

And that was it. Emergency over.

"Nice," said Erdovan in Irfan's ears. "Perfect."

The young SpitRider's entire head was buzzing. "Thanks, Dad," he managed to mutter, through numb lips. All his movements had slowed to a crawl as his body struggled to recover from the extreme accelerations it had experienced. Only his brain was still operating at full throttle. Five-point-seven minutes had passed since the emergency began. It would take him forty-seven seconds to return to Dock. Followed by another ten to slip into position. His heart was pounding.

But his father wanted to talk. "You know, son, if you keep this up I might be able to . . ."

Irfan's fingers were keying in the entry code to his class. "All *right*, Dad," he said, trying not to let his impatience show. Respect to elders was considered a security issue on space stations.

"Son, I don't think you appreciate the importance of advancing quickly within the system. You don't want to be stuck forever hauling Spit, do you?"

No, of course not, Dad! thought Irfan. *Now please! Let me go!*

"Reaching your level is all very well. But rack up your bonuses and you could shave a whole month from your annual work quota!"

"Dad," said Irfan. "I've got my class?" He'd missed six minutes already. SIX. MINUTES.

"Class?"

"Home Languages. Look—"

"*Language class?* But you're already fluent! It's a waste of time! You don't need to learn—"

"Dad!" Irfan cut in. "I'm GOING!" And he switched off his headset.

The bliss of silence. Plus the faint ping of the remote server as it tuned into the lesson.

In front of him, through the pod's skin, the velvet blackness of space had been restored, with its pinpricks of light representing the light of distant suns. Each tiny twinkle was enhanced with glowing numbers and positioning data. It was like looking out onto his own private patch of eternity.

Between Irfan and the curving interior surface of the pod's hull was the crescent-shaped console on which his keypad and other controls were located. It was an "intelligent" surface; it looked and felt like a physical console, but was actually a projection. When the remote server beeped to announce that the session was about to begin, the console glowed, then filmed over and grew a smooth platform that floated a centimeter above it.

A small, graceful figure appeared on the platform. A girl. A very pretty girl. She wore a simple costume made of a lightweight flowing material that left her arms and legs bare. Her dark hair was caught in a ponytail. Even though the entire projection was less than thirty centimeters tall, it was diamond clear. Irfan could make out her microscopic eyelashes. The shadow cast by her eyelashes on her cheeks. The dot of light on her pink lips.

Leila. Her name was Leila. And she was his personal Home Languages assistant.

"You're late." But she was smiling. She never got angry.

"I . . . I'm sorry," stammered Irfan. "There was an incoming alert ten seconds before class—"

"Wow. That means you dealt with it in . . . *six minutes*? You are amazing!"

"Five-point-seven, actually," said Irfan, feeling his cheeks flush. Now he was showing off. "It takes a while to recover from the recoil. And stuff. Plus I had to return to dock."

"It's awesome. What you SpitRiders do. We're all so grateful to you."

"You don't have to be," said Irfan at once. "It's why we're here."

That was the literal truth. His parents, both of whom were astronauts, had been chosen for a mission that required them to have children during the long journey from Earth to Saturn. The first of these offspring would be in their teens by the time they arrived within Saturn9's orbit, having trained all along the way to become SpitRiders. It was a desperate measure and had been controversial in its time, but it revealed the extreme value placed on Saturnium.

"That doesn't make it any less amazing. You're just fifteen. And already a hero."

Irfan glowed.

"Anyway," continued Leila. "Let's get to the lesson. Do you have questions for me?"

"Yes," said Irfan. "The segment I watched was set in the twenty-first century. It was filmed at a . . . *school*?" He had never seen gatherings of more than fifteen children at any time in his life. His siblings and two other families were the only children present on his home station. There were other stations ringing the moon, of course, but face-to-face meetings were impractical.

"Right," said Leila. "School was where children met in order to learn things."

"Well, there's a word they kept using," said Irfan. "I looked it up. It means 'low temperature.' But the way they used the word didn't make sense!"

Leila smiled. "You mean, 'cool'?"

"Yes," said Irfan. "I'm guessing it's because they didn't have climate controls in their homes? It was very hot?"

Leila's smile broadened. "No! They were talking about a state of mind. An attitude. To be called 'cool' was considered a great compliment. Like being 'cool-headed' under pressure. Like you are, when you collect Spit—"

"*Me?*" exclaimed Irfan. "No way! I'm not cool—I have the most *boring life*! All I do is collect Spit! And listen to my Dad talk about *bonuses*! With *nothing* to look forward to but . . ." He paused. "Meeting you."

"Hmmm," said Leila, pursing her lips and frowning. "Irfan, I told you already: it's not healthy for you to feel that way about me."

Irfan drew in his breath. "I thought about what you said, Miss Leila." He felt ridiculous. His face was hot. His voice was sliding up and down like a yo-yo. "I'm sorry, but I disagree. I really loved what we did the other day. I really, *really* want to do it again."

"But I'm only a virtual teaching assistant, right?" said Leila. "I'm not flesh and blood."

"I know," said Irfan. "And it makes no difference. Ever since the last lesson, I haven't stopped thinking about you." He covered the visor of his helmet with his hands. "If we can't go on meeting, Miss Leila . . . I . . . I don't know what I'll do!"

Leila paused. "Listen to me, Irfan, have you ever thought about what you *actually* do? As a SpitRider?"

"I told you, SpitRiding is nothing," he said. "It's boring and—"

"No! I meant, d'you ever think about what happens to Spit? When it gets back to Earth?"

He nodded his head glumly. Sure, he knew what happened. It just didn't seem a big deal though. Not for him, not at this distance.

"It's converted into the cleanest, safest, and most efficient form of fuel ever known. The earth is no longer polluted because of Saturnium. Everyone, everywhere is safer and healthier. And it's all made possible because of incredibly brave and clever people like—well, *you!*"

Irfan made a face. "Okay. If you say so. But I don't want to be brave or clever, Miss Leila. I want . . ." He sighed. "Please! I want to be virtual with you again."

There was a pause. Then it was Leila's time to sigh. "All right, then. Come on. We've got barely nine minutes." Irfan's fingers were already tapping codes onto the platform on which Leila stood. "I've signed you in."

Seconds later, there were two small gleaming figures on the virtual platform above Irfan's console. Irfan's avatar wore a formal dress suit, while Leila wore a long, graceful gown, pearly white in color. Leila took his hands and positioned them so that one was on her shoulder and the other was on her waist. From the speakers, the opening bars of *The Blue Danube* welled out.

"The waltz again! You're sure?" asked Leila, as she began to move, leading Irfan with expert steps. "You wouldn't like to try something else?"

"Oh no," said Irfan, his eyes shining. "*This* is what I want. Can't get enough of it!"

Leila laughed. "You know those school students? In the clip? If they could see you now, they'd be blown away! In that era, dancing a waltz with your teacher was considered the absolute screaming opposite of being cool."

Irfan shrugged.

"I don't care," he said, as they twirled against the backdrop of distant suns.

I am connected to the planet by strings of molecules. Between my toes and the coast of Africa is a sheet of water molecules. Africa is home to Ostrich, to whom legend has been quite unfair—

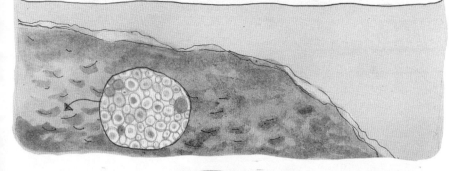

Ostrich buries his head in sand not out of cowardice or denial, but because he is quite toothless—

and must swallow pebbles to serve as gastroliths to grind food in his gizzard.

My parents turn to the great outdoors for inspiration and analogy. No surprise, given my Nat Geo nomenclature. Mom had this to say about navigating moody female friendships:

In a beehive, first thing a young queen does is assassinate other young queens.

Comparisons to the plot of "Mean Girls" are valid. To be a queen who won't bump off competition is a mutation, not a norm.

You're a mutant queen.

The trick, it seems, is to be autonomous without morphing into an evil-tempered wasp.

They'll flock to you when you can love and not want anything back.

When I stopped waiting for return gifts from the world, I found my appetite. You couldn't tell from looking at my plate, but I got the biggest appetite you'll know. Food is the least of it.

Food-hunger is easily sated; its aftermath is drowsiness. I eat gratefully but moderately. What I don't consume in moderation is life. Fill me with the world. Topography, sound, water, fruit, pigment, plankton, soil, spore, spice, space—

You're full of shit, Coral!

That too!

Omit nothing. I'll take the refuse. Humus, ash, bones, sweet rot that will nourish land, grain, and—in extension—all the animals that graze. If I could, I'd ingest and neutralize toxins. I'll take it all.

I promise to offer a less dank dwelling place than the inside of a whale!

A biblical lad named Jonah was swallowed by a whale. In the distended belly, Jonah remained for 3 days. Until he saw sense, and until the whale sifted out the plankton from the brine.

You hear tales of wolf-bellied heroes, of demons who eat rice by the cartload. When Krishna's mother pried his mouth open, she saw the multiverse curling inside.

Hard to handle? I'll erase this memory.

Appetite is such a boys' club. Egypt's sky goddess, Nut, arches over the world, but does not contain it. Her belly is politely taut.

Female bellies are allowed their moon curves only when swollen with baby.

As I understand and assimilate more of the world inside me, the plan is to avoid bloating in an ungainly, possessive lump but to grow easy, spacious. May I stretch, discard old outlines. May my perimeters grow vast and porous—
with sunlight streaming in. I'd look like a zeppelin.
And then like a balloon stretched translucent, to bursting point!
Just how bad could that be?

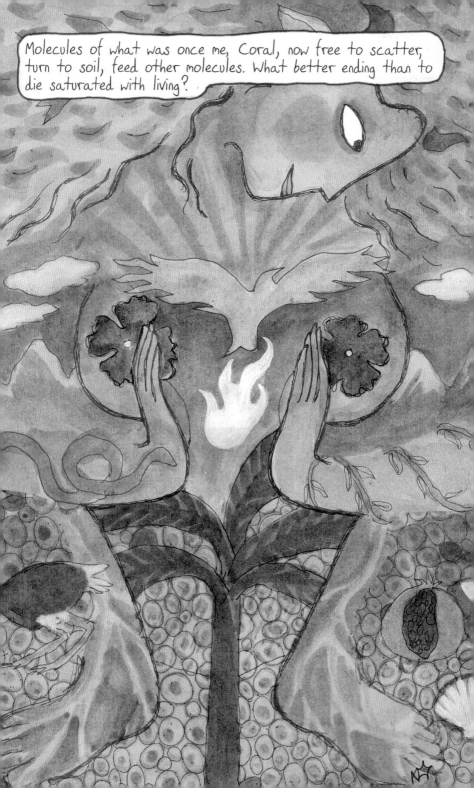

Mirror Perfect

Kirsty Murray

Ettie cringed at the sight of her reflection in the airport concourse windows. With her baby brother, Max, balanced on her hip, she looked like an overweight and exhausted teen mother. She turned her back on the image in the glass as she wrestled with Max, who was eating a hank of her hair that he'd wound around his fat little fist and shoved into his mouth.

Up ahead, Dad had stopped outside an electronics shop. He gazed longingly at its window crammed full of computer devices, while Mila made a high-pitched whining sound and writhed in his arms.

"Don't even think about it, Dad," said Ettie, catching up with him. "We can't take the twins in there. They'll be like kamikaze pilots and dive-bomb every piece of technology in sight. You know what they're like."

"They're exactly like you when you were two."

"No way! I was never into mass destruction like these little monsters. They could cure anyone of ever wanting kids."

Mila reached out for Ettie, despite Ettie's cranky tone. As soon as Dad's grip loosened, the toddler lunged across the space between them and flung her arms around Ettie's neck. Max, inspired by Mila's antics, made a dive for the floor. Ettie lowered them both to the ground, grabbed each of their wrists, and held tight.

"See! You're an excellent kid wrangler, Ettie," said Dad. "Do you think you could manage for five minutes while I check some prices? I'll be quick."

Ettie sighed. The relief on her father's face was like sunshine after a storm.

"You're an angel. I'll meet you at the directory board for Terminal Three in exactly one hour."

"An hour is actually sixty minutes, not five." But her father had disappeared before she finished speaking.

This was not Ettie's idea of a holiday. How could Dad have possibly imagined it was a good idea to take twin two-year-olds on a vacation that involved a twenty-three-hour flight and a five-hour layover in an international airport? It was the sort of torture designed to make Ettie wish she were an only child.

Ettie glanced down the long, shining mall. Thousands of people were moving along the concourse. Some were dragging suitcases, others browsing the shops, while further along the aisle, weary passengers were lying slumped or stretched out asleep in the lounge areas.

Ettie stopped in front of a display of brightly colored clothes in a shop window.

"I guess you can't do too much damage in a clothing shop," she said hopefully.

She led the twins inside and kept them firmly corralled between her legs and a shelf of neatly folded T-shirts. When she'd picked out a couple of pale blue tops, she maneuvered the twins into a changing room cubicle. The woman at the counter glared at her, but Ettie felt sure that if the twins would just sit by her feet for a few minutes, she could quickly try on the T-shirts.

Max and Mila pressed their faces against the mirror in the changing booth and smiled at themselves. They licked the glass as if nothing tasted as good as their own reflections. Looming above them, Ettie stared at herself. The harsh glare of the fluorescent light made her skin seem blotchy; there was a new pimple on her cheek, and her hair looked oily and lank. Her jeans were too tight and she pinched the flesh above her hips with irritation and tugged at her bra, trying to straighten out her clothes so she wouldn't look so lumpy. She was almost jealous of the way the twins admired their reflections. She hated her own. Her eyes were too far apart, her nose was too long, and she loathed the dimple in her chin. She couldn't remember the last time she'd looked in the mirror and liked what she'd seen. Had she ever been like Max and Mila, so admiring, so excited about the image the glass presented? The mirror seemed to flicker and gleam at her, throwing back the ugliest version of herself possible.

The twins were perfectly content to play with their reflections as Ettie peeled off her hoodie. It was only when she had her hands trapped in the long sleeves that she realized what a mistake she'd made. Suddenly, Mila dived under the door of the changing booth and scuttled across the smooth tiles. Max followed her, even though Ettie clumsily tried to grab him by the ankle.

By the time she had shed her hoodie and thrown the door of the changing booth open, the twins were out of sight. She felt a momentary panic until she heard the shop attendant shouting. Max had pulled a pink silk scarf from a rack and was trailing it behind him while he pawed at a display of feathery accessories. Mila was almost out the door, her stubborn little head down as she tugged and pulled at the hem of a black satin dress worn by the mannequin in the window display.

After apologizing and wrestling the twins into her arms, Ettie gave up on the idea of shopping.

"One hour! What am I going to do with you for one whole hour?"

She wandered up the concourse to the information area, tugging on the twins' tiny wrists as they squealed and giggled. Then they both went limp, dragging their knees across the smooth marble floor, forcing Ettie to pull their full weight.

Although the plush red seats looked comfortable, she kept away from them. The last thing she needed was for

Max to wipe his nose on the textured velour and provoke someone else to glare at her. She stopped and studied the airport map. There were six terminals and hundreds of shops, restaurants, and cafes, but nowhere that seemed safe when you had a pair of rampaging toddlers to manage.

"What about the butterfly enclosure?" she said, squatting down beside Max and Mila. "Would you like to see the butterflies flutter by?" she asked, tickling Max under the chin.

Mila put her hands out and wiggled her fingers, "Budder-by," she said. Max laughed, "Budder-by," and then they both reached their hands up and clapped them together. "Swash 'em," they shouted with glee. "Munch 'em."

"No, you bad babies. No swashing budder-bys on my watch. And definitely no munching." The twins crowed with laughter and Ettie turned back to studying the map.

She wondered if Dad had factored in how long it was going to take them to get to Gate 137 to catch their next flight. She traced her finger along the grid of light rail that connected the terminals. It took seventeen minutes to get from Terminal 3 to Terminal 6. If she took the twins for a ride down to the gate, she could scout out exactly how long the round trip would take and still be back in time to meet up with Dad. At least it would keep the diabolic duo on the move.

"Okay, team," she said. "Let's check out how fast we can nail this trip."

She found the long glass tube that was the light-rail station for Terminal 3. The doors slid open and a crowd of travelers with carry-on luggage surged into the train. Ettie herded the twins into a corner, away from the other travelers. At each terminal, the train disgorged passengers. By the time they left Terminal 5, the carriage was empty but for Ettie and the twins. Max began to whine, and Mila found her porta-cup in Ettie's carry bag and tipped the contents onto the floor.

"Mila!" said Ettie. "Naughty!"

Suddenly, the lights of the carriage flickered and died. They were plunged into darkness. The twins let out a simultaneous wail, and Ettie let go of the safety rail and drew the toddlers tightly against her. "It's okay," she said. "It's just a power surge."

But the train kept hurtling into the darkness. Ettie fumbled for her mobile phone and flicked it on. It cast a pale light across the frightened faces of the twins, but it didn't pick up a signal.

"Terminal Seven," said the computerized announcer in Chinese, Spanish, English, Hindi, and Arabic. "You are now arriving at Terminal Seven."

"What happened to Terminal Six?" Ettie asked the empty carriage as the lights surged back on and the train stopped. "Maybe we should just stay on board until it goes back."

As if the announcer had heard her comment, the automated voice said, "This train is terminating at Terminal Seven. Please disembark immediately."

The doors slid open and Ettie and the twins stepped onto the platform. Terminal 7 didn't look very different from Terminal 3, except it was eerily uninhabited.

The shops opposite were all shut, their windows dark. Ettie's reflection in the black glass was disfigured by undulations in the surface. Even as she stared, her torso seemed to swell. She stepped closer and the image changed again, her belly ballooning as if she were pregnant, her face growing long and tired. The faces of the twins, distorted, grew rounder and pale, their open mouths like gaping maws, their eyes black holes in their faces. Ettie shuddered.

They walked slowly toward the brightly lit concourse of gleaming floors and high walls of glass, but not a single traveler was in sight. There wasn't even any music playing in the background, and Ettie was unnerved by the sound of their feet slapping on the glittering stone. The information booth was empty, so she stopped briefly to study the terminal map for a light-rail timetable, but there was no timetable and the map was enormous, as if Terminal 7 was a city in itself.

The twins began to whimper and Ettie's arms ached from dragging them around. Beside the terminal map was a line of gleaming steel trolleys. There were baby strollers too, including a sleek, silver, rocket-shaped one especially designed for two. Ettie had never seen a stroller like it. Instead of one baby having to sit behind or on top of the other, the twins could sit facing each other. She unhooked it from the row and it glided smoothly into her grasp.

"Perfect," said Ettie. She dumped Mila into a seat and strapped Max into the opposite side.

The stroller seemed to grow suddenly heavy, as if the

wheels were made of lead, or gravity had altered. Ettie wiped away sweat that beaded on her forehead, put her head down, and doggedly maneuvered the stroller into the main concourse.

The shops glowed, a soft light emanating from each window. Ettie was relieved to see that some of them were open. Cool air wafted from the entrances, but instead of the ghastly glare of the Terminal 3 shops, the interiors were golden and warm. Ettie caught her reflection in a shop window and stopped the stroller. The lighting was much more flattering here. Her skin looked smooth and flawless, her limbs appeared slimmer, her hips neater. She smiled and the gap between her teeth and the crookedness of them hardly seemed to matter at all. The scar above her left eye, the thin silvery line where she'd bumped her head on the table when she was three, had disappeared. Her long black hair looked silkier, her breasts fuller, the lumps and bumps of her hips and thighs pared down and svelte. If only she looked like this in every mirror, life would be so much easier.

Checking that the twins couldn't escape, she parked the stroller outside the nearest open boutique clothing store and then stepped inside.

A tall, thin blonde stood at the counter, staring at a screen behind the cash register, her expression transfixed, like a mannequin's, but her presence reassured Ettie. A heavy bassline throbbed through the speakers inside the shop, even though Ettie hadn't been able to hear it when she was walking down the main arcade of the terminal. She drifted between the aisles of clothes and picked out an armful of skimpy tops and a pair of very short orange shorts. She'd normally never try on clothes that were so revealing, but the image of herself in every mirror made her feel more confident.

In the changing room, she was startled by what she saw. The girl in the mirror was perfect, sleek and sexy, her skin smooth, her eyes sparkling. Even the pimple on her cheek had vanished. She touched the mirror and the glass felt warm and soft, her fingers sinking slightly into its surface, as if the mirror wanted to suck her fingertips, to taste her beauty. She snatched her hand away, but she could still feel the pull of the mirror, like a magnet, drawing her to it. Her knees made contact with the glass and then her face. She was slipping into her own reflection and it felt wonderful. But suddenly, like a tiny spark in the back of her brain, a throb in the pit of her belly, she thought of the twins.

Ettie stepped back, threw open the changing room door and ran out of the shop. She was sure she'd parked the stroller to the left of the shop's entrance, but it was nowhere in sight. She broke into a run. The air seemed heavier, holding her back, and her feet felt as if they were encased in concrete.

She shouted, "Max, Mila, Max, Mila!" Her voice echoed against the atrium ceiling and came back to her like the screech of a wild bird.

From far away, she heard a sound like two cats howling, and she knew it was the twins. A flicker of movement caused her to spin around in time to see the rocket-shaped stroller hurtling down toward a pair of sliding doors beyond which lay a fiery gateway.

"Final boarding call, final boarding call . . ." boomed a voice.

"No!" shouted Ettie.

She took a deep breath and plunged through the thick air, gaining ground on the stroller. With her last ounce of strength, she leaped into the air, diving to catch the handle before it could glide through the sliding doors. The stroller fell on its side and Ettie wrenched it roughly toward her. The straps that held the twins in place snapped and they tumbled out onto the floor. They scrambled toward her and she swept the toddlers into her arms, clinging to them tightly. They were whimpering now, beyond screams.

"Don't worry. I won't let anyone take you from me."

Ettie turned and ran through the glittering arcade, back to the light-rail terminal. She caught her reflection in the mirrors as she ran. Her arms and legs had grown thick again, her black hair had lost its gloss and was matted and tangled. She didn't stop. She kept running, running until she reached the light-rail. To her relief, a train was drawing into the station. She elbowed the button by the doorway, not wanting to risk letting go of the twins. Nothing happened. She kicked the door and bellowed at the top of her voice, a wordless sound that contained all her rage.

The glass doors slid back and she jumped into the carriage. Ettie collapsed onto a seat, the twins held fast against her chest. They pressed their cheeks against hers and for the first time since leaving home, Ettie realized how much she loved them.

As the train pulled out of the station, she glanced back at Terminal 7. A dark-haired girl stood on the platform, staring at them as they disappeared from view. Ettie stared back. The girl was a mirror image of Ettie, the flawless, perfect version, a beautiful mannequin with a vacant expression.

Arctic Light

Vandana Singh

I was let out of prison on my seventeenth birthday. That was yesterday.

Eight months ago I was a different person. Everything was different. There was, for instance, the light of sun on snow, the endless sea, the sky of the Arctic. I thought I was brave, a rebel taking on the greatest cause in the history of humankind. On the ship *Valiant*, sailing from northern Canada to the East Siberian Sea, the light reminded me of a certain look I remembered in my mother's eyes. Angry as I was with the world, I felt a kind of peace here, a momentary easing of breath.

I remember, when we got to our destination, how the oil rig was a tiny blip in the border between sea and sky, a crooked arm raised up, a scarecrow. TundraSaur's rig was only the second major oil-drilling operation in the Arctic, but the world's oil companies were desperately scrambling for permits to start drilling. Beside me on the deck, Natalia stared at the shoreline of her country, her jaw set. Her hair was streaked with gray, and there was a scar on her jawbone shaped like a sword. She had led several protests in Russia and had been in prison twice. We had barely spoken to each other for the past three days—she was angry with me for insisting I would take part in the action, and had told me horror stories of prison life. Her anger was no match for my obstinacy, although if I hadn't lied about my age the others would not have supported me. Tentatively I reached out and pressed her hand where it clutched the railing. She didn't look at me or smile, just nodded, patted my hand, and went inside. A truce of sorts.

We dropped anchor just outside Russian waters. Now the rig loomed large before us. There were four security boats reconnoitering the waters around it. Natalia spoke to them in rapid Russian over the radio. "We come in peace," she said, "to protest the drilling for oil in the Arctic. We are currently at anchor in international waters."

A man replied belligerently in Russian.

"He's just warning us we'll be arrested if we enter Russian waters," Natalia said. Now the game was afoot.

The night before the action felt to me like the last night in the world. I had volunteered to be among those courting arrest because I wanted to bring climate change to the attention of the Indian public. Although there was a national action plan on climate, the government was building coal-fired power plants as though there was no tomorrow. (With that much fossil fuel being burned, there wouldn't be.) All the work of scientists like my mother, all their warnings, had come to nothing. Reading the news about cyclones and floods, heat waves and freak storms was bad enough. When the sea came for Mumbai, breaching the new sea wall and sweeping away the familiar streets of my childhood, it brought horrors from which even Fahad Uncle couldn't protect me. I was haunted—by my mother's eyes, when she lay dying, by the memory of walking through waist-deep floodwaters, terrified I'd be swept away. In my nightmares I heard the roar of the water, felt Mona's hand slip from mine, again and again. Fahad Uncle shouted, grabbed me, made a leap for her, but the current was too strong. There were snakes in the water, and the distended bodies of slum children, and, once, a pink plastic doll with bright orange hair, smiling maniacally. Three years later there are still nights I can't sleep.

But that last night before the action, I was awake for a different reason. My responsibility was to help unleash the webstorm, an extreme cyberweather event that would come in like a cyclone, sweeping into other conversations and connections, not by force but by the power of social media and crazy network geometry. I was crazy-network-geometry girl, on deck with my laptop and twitchy fingers, waiting for our tech team to let the drones go.

The drone lights were dimmed to a barely perceptible glow. We sent them off fondly, with a bottle or two of wine. On my screen you could see the locations of the drones, little yellow blinking lights, the seeing eyes of the world. With a touch of my finger, the Million Eyes Inner Collective around the world woke up in Dhaka and Rangoon, Boston and Vladivostok, Oslo and Berlin. Questions and answers popped on the screen like firecrackers.

We can't see anything!

Well, it's night over there, moron!

I see some lights! Is that the rig?

No, it's effing aliens. Of course it is the rig.

We go worldwide as soon as action starts in the morning.

That morning, Natalia and I and Fabio and Aarne got in the little boat with the banner and the megaphone. In the cold predawn light, with pink streaks in the eastern sky, the water was very still, as though the world was waiting. We could hear, faintly, signs of early-morning activity on the rig, and someone on one of the security boats calling out. Our boat was so small they didn't see us until we were quite close to the platform. We let the banner go. It rose like a ghost while Natalia worked the remote, up and up, until it made contact with the top part of the rig and stayed there. The letters were so huge that you could still see what they said from down below, in English and Russian: *TundraSaur: Continuing the Proud Tradition of Destroying the Earth.*

The confrontation is burned in my memory. I had expected the shouted warning, the security boat looming over us. I didn't expect that we would be so roughly treated. They boarded us and dragged us up onto the deck of their boat. Natalia was yelling something in Russian. Some brute put a hand on her breast and she kicked him in the groin, and then things got bloody. The man who was holding me pulled my head back by my hair and twisted my arms behind me, avoiding my kicking feet. I looked wildly around me and saw through tears that Natalia was handcuffed, blood dripping from her nose, and Aarne and Fabio were both roughed up. Fabio looked furious; Aarne had a deceptive calm on his face, a hint of triumph. He was looking at Natalia, trying to say something with his eyes, and suddenly there was an answering triumph in her own gaze that she immediately covered up. I realized it then, of course. The nearest drone, tiny, stealthy, and barely visible, had video-captured everything. I looked across the expanse of sea to the distant silhouette of our little ship, and saw the glow of the signal that meant: *Webstorm Arctic Light unleashed.*

Fabio shouted for a superior officer. His Russian is pretty good, and it helps that he looks like a bear. I couldn't understand what he or Natalia a moment later were saying, but I knew from our practice sessions. They were talking about the need to respect peaceful protesters' rights, but also about why we were doing what we were doing. Both Fabio and Natalia are trained in oratory—even our brutish captors stopped in their tracks for a moment. Their speeches, via their state-of-the-art wrist computers, were going out to the world in real time.

Ultimately some superior personage came and shouted at our captors, and brought a doctor to attend to Natalia and Fabio (later I learned they had cracked a rib of his—he was orating in quite a bit of pain). Then there was the hustle to get us to cells in the security boat, and finally to a truck onshore that would take us to the nearest big town.

That's how I ended up in prison.

They separated Natalia and me at once. I was shut off from the light, from the sky, from space, crammed into a cell with a woman who stared at me without comprehension. Her hair was tangled around her face—she looked prematurely aged. In all the time I was there, she didn't speak to me even once. The only noises she made were when she snored and when she wept. In the dining halls the women laughed at my poor Russian and teased me about the "Natalia" I was seeking. The food smelled of shoe leather, and the steel doors clanged with a reverberating finality. In that cold, dark place, with the roaches and (I swear) rats running under my bunk, I had no space in my head for anything but despair and horror.

In my third month there, I got sick with a stomach bug that was going around. Tossing in my bunk, or vomiting into the toilet, I longed with feverish desperation to get out, to go back home again, to Fahad Uncle, and maybe even college, and to never, ever see the inside of a prison again.

The Indian consulate sent me a lawyer, a pimply fellow with sly eyes who told me my best bet was to claim I was fifteen, not twenty. I could claim, he said, that my older accomplices had deceived me, manipulated me, forced me to go with them. I'd be out of here in no time. For a moment I thought he'd guessed my age, or close to it—I was sixteen, not fifteen—but my fake passport had taken him in. I stared at him. My stomach was still not recovered, and I was queasy. He mistook my sick, dazed, half-starved look for stupidity. He told me we needed to think through it carefully and he would be back next month.

I lay in my bunk, holding my stomach and trying not to think about throwing up. I couldn't imagine freedom. My cellmate sobbed inconsolably in her bed. I screamed at her, and she stopped and looked vacantly at me. That was worse than her sobbing. I broke down and cried and cried.

An image came to me of the first time we'd field-tested one of the drones, over in northern Canada, before we set off on the *Valiant*. The camera had captured the slow collapse of a young polar bear onto the snowy tundra where it breathed its last frosted breaths, all skin and bone from starvation. That's how I felt now, alone in the world, without hope. There was no point in trying to do anything. My mother had been wrong in trying, and Fahad Uncle, and my friends on the *Valiant*. The oil barons were too powerful. All I had to do when the lawyer came back was to turn against Natalia and the others, as he'd suggested. I thought about how angry Natalia had been with me for courting arrest, and wondered if she'd understand if I betrayed them.

I lay awake. There was grime on the wall by my bunk, and words scratched out in Cyrillic that I couldn't read, but I saw for the first time that someone had taken a hard object and made a crude drawing of a mountain range. It was a reminder that there was a world outside, and there were other people who remembered. I tumbled back in my mind to a certain summer in the Himalayas, when I was thirteen years old.

Imagine me, a small, childish figure standing on an endless field littered with rocks and pebbles—what geologists call a moraine. It slopes up and up toward the ice wall, all the way to the distant white tongue of the glacier. I'm huddled in my parka against the unaccustomed cold, kicking at the rock at my feet. Fahad Uncle and his group are moving around and muttering incomprehensibly, the way scientists do when they are out in the field. This is the last glacier my mother visited before the sickness killed her a year ago. She had been determined to measure unrecorded glacier lengths in the northeastern Himalayas, but she came back about halfway through the planned trip, because she was already sick. I will always remember how she looked at the sky through the hospital window—the murky, polluted city sky—but in her eyes was the light of the Himalayas, the light of sun on snow.

This is the first time her team—now Fahad Uncle's team—has visited this glacier, locally known as the Nilsaya.

Kicking at pebbles, I feel suffused with my mother's presence. The silence here is restful, punctuated only by the muted conversations of the scientists and the distant sharp cracks and groans of the glacier. Then I see, a little ahead of me, a marker protruding from the mess of rocks and pebbles: a metal stake with a tattered little flag atop it.

I run up to it, shouting. The marker's what they've been looking for. The place where the glacier's front edge was, two years ago, as marked by my mother on that last trip.

"Fahad Uncle! Fahad Uncle!"

He's been in my life longer than my father ever was. He has a calm, silent air, rather like a mountain. He gives my shoulder a gentle victory punch as his post-doc student retrieves my mother's last marker and hands it to me.

It's a solemn moment, because I am holding the last thing she touched when she was still mostly whole. But it is also a bit of a shock for us because nobody thought the glacier would have retreated this much in such a short time. Here, where we are standing at this moment, is where that distant cliff of ice was, just two years ago. The remote-sensing equipment has confirmed what our eyes are telling us.

I hold the marker in my hand, and look at the glint of sun on the glacier so far up the slope. My fears rise around me in a dark wave, and the dam breaks. I weep as though I will never stop.

Fahad Uncle holds me, says, "Shaila, Shaila." What they don't know is that I am crying not only for my mother, but for the whole world.

That's when I decide: I will join the fight. That is the moment that will bring me, a few eventful years later, to the Arctic. That's before I know about prisons.

* * *

The lawyer didn't come back for two months, and then only because the webstorm had generated enough worldwide outrage. He told me the UN had held a special session about Arctic drilling, and there were protests in the streets all over the world. In India, the youth climate movement was taking off as never before—they had stalled three coal power plants, and were clamoring for my release. My friends on the *Valiant* were on hunger strike. The lawyer related the news with an air of faint distaste, as though all this was beneath him. The thought that there were people outside trying to get me out made tears come into my eyes. When the lawyer began outlining his strategy, I decided I hated his sly eyes and his condescension. With a spurt of my old anger I told him to get lost. I was breathing so hard, I thought I would pass out. But the anger did me some good—it cut through my despair. How I survived the remaining months, I don't know, but it must have had something to do with my rage, and the memory of light.

Yesterday they let us go. I spent eight months in a Russian prison, and my birthday present was my freedom. I stepped out of the courthouse, momentarily blinded by the brightness of the day. I breathed in great gulps of fresh air. There were red and yellow flowers blooming in the square. And there was Fahad Uncle, unfamiliar in a Russian-style hat, fighting through the crowds toward me, shouting and waving. After the tears and hugs, he handed me something.

"You should have this," he said.

I unwound the cloth from the small bundle he handed me. A battered little metal marker, the tattered flag. My mother's last scientific act: the stake in the ground, the declaring of a boundary, a catastrophe, a limit. But also, maybe, a gauntlet.

We walked together toward the taxi stand. My mobile phone (recently returned to me) beeped: a message from Captain Bill on the *Valiant*, congratulating me on my release. An unspoken question hung in the air. I thought of the sun on snow, and felt my mother beside me as though she had never left.

I took a deep breath. I would go home for a while, remember how to live in the world again. And then—

I'll be back, I texted him, and followed Fahad Uncle to the taxi.

THE RUNNERS

Isobelle CARMODY
and **Prabha MALLYA**

In the Time Before, Men and Boys were not free. They were owned in a world ruled by the Mothers.

Pack food for a journey, Boy.

If there is need for speed, Miladi, I can summon the kitchenBoy.

Stop talking. Get the food.

Put these on.

But Miladi, this is not correct attire for a HelpMate.

Obey me, and call me Geneva... I will call you Hel.

That is what you called me when you were a child.

That was my mother's fault for making me believe you were human.

I am not authorized to leave Homeground!

I order you to leave Homeground.

I AM MAYA 7 OF HOMESAFE. I AM THE LAST WOMAN STANDING. I WAS LEFT TO GUARD THE WAY.

15:38 070001256

You are one of the synthetic Women created by true men!

PROCESSING....

I AM SHE WHO WAITS. BUT YOU ARE THE FIRST WHO EVER CAME.

What about the true men who made the tunnel and built this place?

THE MAN WHO MADE ME WAS KILLED BY THE AMAZONS, AS WERE ALL HIS SISTERS.

Do you know the way to the Promised Land?

MAYA7

THERE IS NO PROMISED LAND.

THE SISTERS WERE GOING TO MAKE ONE AND SEND COORDINATES BACK, BUT THE AMAZONS CAME BEFORE THEY COULD DO IT...

The true men and their sisters dreamed of a Promised Land. Is it possible the stories we heard just grew from that?

Geneva, you must eat and drink. I will prepare it. Maya 7, is there food here?

THERE IS FOOD FOR HUMANS, BUT YOU ...

I hated it when my mother said she was your mother too, because part of her had gone into you.

Biological matter is used to create Men and Boys, but it does not make us human.

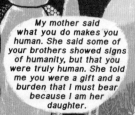

My mother said what you do makes you human. She said some of your brothers showed signs of humanity, but that you were truly human. She told me you were a gift and a burden that I must bear because I am her daughter.

nnnn

[target acquired]

ZNNN
ZNNN
ZNNN
ZNNN

HEL!!

Run, Geneva. Return to Mother City before you are killed.

No!

But you will die if I take it out!

I have to get you to a biodoc!

No. Even if they did not destroy me, they would remove my mind chip and strip out my memories.

The Blooming

A story in the form of a play script

Manjula Padmanabhan and Kirsty Murray

CHARACTERS:

SCHAUM—teenage dweller of the distant planet MaggiNoo, looks like an enormous mass of softly quivering, translucent tentacles. Study Partner of JERK.

JERK—spotty-faced human teenager, daughter of Colonial Federation Officer. Wears slime-wrap sheath, hair made up in purple cones.

LEX and LOU—acrobatic, child-sized human clones, wearing shimmering gray one-piece suits.

CHORUS (THE HERD)—human clones who have outlived their work potential. They are dressed in drab gray overalls, and wander the planet chanting rhymes.

[SFX: water dripping, crackling, electronic buzzing]

The stage is bathed in indigo light. Tiny random flashes ripple continuously across the room like horizontal lightning.

The walls, floor, and ceiling are soft and knobbly, filled with giant protrusions that hang down from above and thrust up from below and on all sides.

At stage front is a gigantic flat panel, six meters wide, four meters tall. It's a dual screen communication monitor. The side facing the audience is idle. SCHAUM is facing the audience seated behind the panel and partially obscured from view. All we see is a mound of delicate tentacles, tapering toward pale pink tips.

The indigo light that bathes the room emanates from SCHAUM's side of the monitor.

SCHAUM: (*speaking through a translator-bot*) Oooh . . . (*crackles, static*) . . . I can't do this. My Study Partner's late. Again. She has no regard for my time. She disrespects me in every way. Why must we work together? Why pretend that we can ever be friends? Of course we cannot! She hates me for being soft-bodied and intuitive, for my intangible pleasures and multisensory abilities. I hate her for her bony limbs, her clumsy, rigid reasoning processes, her tiny pinhole eyes. Everything about these vertebrates—

Offstage—laughter. LEX cartwheels onto the stage, stops in front of the panel, does a series of handsprings followed by a pratfall, then lies completely still.

SCHAUM: (*raising a tentacle or two, to scan the intruder using its sensitive tips*) Hah! With any luck it has snapped its flimsy little neck.

LOU slopes out of the shadows and kneels down beside the prostrate LEX. Pats her cheek and gently brushes her bangs to one side.

LOU: Get up! Don't tease Noodle Head.

LEX: (*sits up, grinning*) Awww. You're no fun. I wanted to make it panic!

LOU: It hardly sounds like it's panicking.

LEX: It said that we're clumsy. I can understand it thinking that about Big-Ups like Jerk—but you and me? Nahhh.

The monitor blinks on. An image of JERK appears, enormously enlarged.

JERK: Hey, NOODLE-LIMBS—I heard what you said. And guess what? I'm going to report you for cultural intolerance! We vertebrates are only your humble colonizers, you know? And guess why? 'Cause these bony limbs you hate so much can STOMP your entire wriggling mass to PULP!!

SCHAUM: (*crackling*) BOTTOM-FEEDERS! POTTY-SUCKERS! (*static*) If not for our invaluable dung, which your worthless species can use as rocket fuel, you wouldn't be within twelve hundred light years of us!

LOU: (*whispering*) Sheesh! Seems like we've wandered into the Insult Olympics...

LEX: (*not bothering to whisper*) Never mind them—c'mon, let's practice cartwheels.

LEX and LOU begin cavorting about.

JERK: Hey! Who let you in here, you undersized squirts? You're distracting my Study Partner. If you're not careful, Laksa-limbs will imprint you and we'll all be reported—

LEX: Imprint? Squash us, you mean?

JERK: No, you ignoramus! The MaggiNoos have mind-control. Get too close to one of 'em and you'll become its slave, following it around like a brainless duckling!

SCHAUM: (*crackles*) Huh! Why would I bother to imprint *vertebrates*? You have no qualities that we admire, no cultural insights to share with us—

Just then, the CHORUS shuffles onstage, six from stage left, six from stage right, slow-moving and hesitant.

JERK: Ohhhh . . . no, no, NO! Here comes the Idiot Herd! Now we'll *never* get this assignment finished tonight!

The screen flickers and breaks into pixels. JERK fades from view.

SCHAUM: Oi! She's gone again—and why are the noise-makers here? Why doesn't anyone explain anything? Ohhhhh! VERTEBRATES! Hateful, despicable . . .

CHORUS: (*singing in unison in a flat monotone to the tune of "Girls and Boys Come Out to Play"*) Boys and girls come out to play, the moon doth shine as bright as day, leave your supper and leave your sleep, and come with your playmates into the street . . .

SCHAUM: . . . cruel . . . (*soft hiccuping sobs*) . . . inconsiderate . . .

LEX: (*frowning*) Do you ever wonder why they sing that song?

LOU: Not really. They creep me out.

LEX: I hope we don't wind up like them—

LOU: Does it make you wonder what will happen to us?

LEX: What do you mean?

LOU: You know, are we going to turn into boys? Or girls? Or wind up in The Herd?

LEX and LOU turn to stare at the CHORUS as the two groups pass each other and exit on opposite sides, continuing to sing all the while.

SCHAUM: (*addressing no one in particular*) First, they occupy our planet for their benefit but pretend we're all working together for Universal Peace. Then they force us to study together to share cultural knowledge, but they're rude and threatening. Then (*sobs*) they permit noisy performers to wander at will through our homes, frightening us with their stamping feet! Now I'm a mass of nerves and my Study Partner's vanished and the assignment will not be completed at all. But who will suffer? Who will be punished? Me! Only me!

LEX: (*finally noticing SCHAUM's distress*) Eh? Hey, hey, hey! Wait. (to LOU) Noodle Head is crying.

LOU: That's not right. We should help it—or her, rather. She *is* a her, isn't she?

LEX: Oh, that's right! The MaggiNoodlies are all female. (*with a bounce, she leaps up and perches along the top edge of the panel*) Yoo-hoo! Noodlie-doo? Up here. Look. Don't cry. Maybe we can help you?

LOU: (*also bouncing up*) We vertebrates aren't all the same, you know. Some of us can even be nice.

LEX: Like us, for instance. We're nice. Unlike the Big-Ups.
SCHAUM: Ohhh. Why should I believe you? Body shape IS destiny. You lot, with your rigid internal structures, are INCAPABLE of flexibility, tact, and understanding. Whereas we . . . (*gives way to grief*)

LOU and LEX stand together, staring down toward SCHAUM from their perch atop the panel.

LOU: (*to LEX*) Y'know? I feel like we should give her a hug.
LEX: But which bit of her is huggable? (*she jumps down off the panel*)
LOU: Wait for me! (*jumps down as well*)

The monitor flickers as JERK returns.

JERK: What? You're still here? Go away—scat! You don't have permission to be inside my study zone. You're distracting my study specimen.
LOU: Schaum isn't a specimen. She has feelings and you've been mean and made her cry.
LEX: We want to hug her and help her to feel better.
JERK: Forget it! Feelings are for higher beings—like us. These creatures are more like worms, or bugs or . . . or . . . jellyfish. That's why we're superior to them. 'Cause we have two genders and real parents and nice, hard skeletons.
LEX: I don't have any parents and I'm not going to have ANY gender. I'm never going to turn into a girl, or a boy. I'm going to stay being me—just Lex—forever.
JERK: (*laughing*) What a witless tadpole you are! Look under

your clothes and you'll find that you're a girl. In another three months, you'll turn into a woman and be sent off to the kitchens. Lou is a boy. He'll turn into a man and be sent off to the war effort. That's what happens to squirts like you. Either that or you'll both wind up in a Herd.

LEX: That's not true! You're making things up, trying to scare us. Just because you're a Big-Up doesn't mean you know everything. Me and Lou aren't gendered yet—

JERK: (*laughing harder*) Dimwitches. Fail-geeks. You don't even know your gender orientation!

SCHAUM: (*her voice is crackling and sparking at the edges*) I . . . I'm sorry, I don't understand. Are you saying (*she lifts a tentacle and pokes it at LEX*) that you and . . . and . . . my Study Partner are not of one mind? Vertebrates have disagreements amongst one another?

LEX: Oi . . . That's my plexus you just solared! (*but she's not harmed. She catches the tip of the tentacle in both hands. She is unsure what rules of etiquette govern the holding of tentacles with an alien entity.*)

LOU: Ohhh. You don't know the half of it, Noodle Head. The colonial fathers who came to your planet brought along half-sized clones—

JERK: Shut up, *shut up*, little nitwits—

LEX: That is, clones like us. We're the size of human children— (*continues holding the tentacle*)

LOU: —brought here as a race of underlings. To do boring, labor-intensive tasks in the colonies. Meanwhile our Superiors—like your friend Jerk—are free to be . . . Superior! They're bigger and stronger than us. We call them Big-Ups.

JERK: *Stop!* Information about our cloning policies is strictly classified!

LEX: —except we won't grow much taller or heavier. Even when we're fully grown.

LOU: Basically, the Big-Ups think of us as living machines. Expendable.

JERK: This is going to end very badly for you—whatever your names are—Loo-Loo and Laxative?

SCHAUM: This is all very new to me. I had no idea your species were differentiated socially.

JERK: Very badly indeed. I'm alerting my dad right now. We'll soon see who has the last laugh!

Screen blinks off again.

SCHAUM: What about the others who came through here, the screeching team?

LEX: The Herd, we call them. They're half-sized clones like us, but they can't work anymore. They've lost muscle tone and motivation. So all they can do is wander about singing. Trying to be jolly.

CHORUS: *(singing offstage)* Clones don't eat and clones can't play. We have seen neither moon nor day. Clear the dung and heap it high. We must work or we will die . . .

LEX has been holding SCHAUM's tentacle all along, absent-mindedly caressing it.

LOU: Not that they succeed. With the jolliness, I mean.

SCHAUM: I am sensing deep sadness in all that you say.

Amongst my people it is unknown, this kind of soul-disagreement . . . (*she makes an odd sound, something between a tinkle and snort*) Ooo-EEEee! Sorry! I couldn't help myself.

The air within her room begins to fill with softly glowing lights.

SCHAUM: (*raises the tentacle that LEX was holding*) Your . . . uh . . . upper extremities? "Hands"? Your hands are causing a very specialized sensation in my *thrips*! Resulting in an Aura Bloom.

LEX and LOU: (*together, looking around*) Ooooo!

LOU picks up a tentacle and strokes it too, holding it to his cheek. The glowing lights grow more intense.

LEX: I've never seen anything so beautiful.

LOU: And it makes me feel different too. It makes me feel all warm inside. Do you feel it too, Lex?

LEX nods. Both appear bewildered.

CHORUS: (*singing offstage*) Come with a whoop and come with a call, come with a good will or not at all . . .

CHORUS shuffles onstage then hesitates, bewildered by the lights. They stop singing and instead begin to hum in unison.

SCHAUM: What has happened to them? That noise they're making—it's different now. Almost attractive.

The screen flickers and JERK reappears.

JERK: Stop! Turn off your lights! The Herd clones are

changing their tune and they *can't* do that—they'll . . . they'll . . . I dunno! Whatever you're doing to them it's WRONG! You don't have permission—

SCHAUM: I cannot "turn off" an Aura Bloom any more than you can turn on the moon's beams. I am at one with the planet. And your underlings are connected to me. They're amplifying the Bloom. Nothing can stop it.

JERK: Oh, really? Well! My dad's sending a Squad and they'll smash all of you! For breaking the rules—for changing the system—

LOU: Lex, we have to do something. Before the Squad arrives.

LEX: Wait! I have an idea. Hold on tight to Noodle Lady— keep her glowing, quick—

LEX runs over to the CHORUS. She grabs hold of two of the humming clones and draws them toward SCHAUM. Then she picks up a tentacle and places its tip in the arms of first one CHORUS member, then the other.

The Bloom begins to throb.

SCHAUM: This is glorious. I've never felt so intensely alive.

LEX drags another pair of CHORUS members toward SCHAUM and connects them to the tentacles. The lights grow brighter and more intense. A rainbow begins to arc and sway across the stage. The screen flickers on and off.

JERK: Stop it! The power is surging. Whatever you're doing, stop it now! You'll blow the grid!

The CHORUS members relax as they come into contact with SCHAUM's tentacles. They begin to smile and laugh, embracing

the tentacles, wrapping the flexible limbs around themselves.
   In the distance, a bleating alarm.

JERK: Oh no! I can't believe this. We're getting the signal
   to evacuate. This can't be happening. You careless freaks!
   You've not only ruined my study assignment, you've
   destroyed the WHOLE COLONY!

SCHAUM: *(her voice grows deep, rich, and musical)* The
   young ones and I have attained symbiosis. Their
   affection has transformed the biosphere of MaggiNoo.
   From this day forward, our waste products will no longer
   be available to you. If your workers touch our tentacles
   with intent to exploit us, they will be vaporized. The half-
   sized clones are immune from harm, but you and your
   Superiors must leave this planet.

JERK: Nooooooo . . .

The screen flickers and blacks out.

LOU: The Big-Ups are leaving? Lex, you're brilliant!

*LEX punches the air in triumph, does a cartwheel, and then runs
over to join LOU. They both embrace tentacles. The air shimmers,
as an intergalactic aurora borealis forms across the stage. All the
freed child-clones turn their faces to the light in wonder.*

ALL: Aahhhhhhhhhhhh . . . ! *(their voices join in a hymn of
   pure joy, wordless and sweet)*

Lights dim.

CURTAIN

What a Stone Can't Feel

Penni Russon

As far as superpowers go, it's a pretty lame one. I haven't worked out how to *use* it, you know, to fight crime or save the world. I can't even use it to save Bonnie.

What it is, is I go into things. On Sunday, I spent a few hours scooped inside a bowl. Not in the empty part where the ice cream or the cereal goes. I mean *inside* the substance of the bowl. It's sort of a Zen thing. I was the bowl but I was not the bowl. I was me, Vega Sandrine Collins, and I was finest-quality porcelain, dishwasher and microwave safe, made in China. It is very restful being a bowl, once you get used to the sensation of not being yourself. A bowl doesn't want anything. It doesn't love or hurt. You can fill it, empty it, a bowl doesn't care.

* * *

"I've got one," says Jessame.

Lyss and Jessame are Bonnie's cousins. It's the four of us most afternoons. Jessame and Lyss walk in, slipping off their school blazers and casting aside their straw hats, covering the gray-flecked lino floor with their capacious schoolbags emblazoned with the St. Mary of the Cross logo.

I go to Currawong High. Bonnie used to go there too. Back when we thought she was going to get better, I used to tease her that she would fall behind and have to do remedial math and become a mechanic. I don't even bring her homework anymore.

Bonnie smiles her thin, barely there smile, waiting.

Jessame says, "How do you think the world will end?"

"Jessame," groans Lyss.

"Chicken flu? Plague? Something that wipes out humans and leaves the animals to get on with things. That'd be the best."

"Jessame," hisses Lyss.

"What?"

"We're in a hospital. It's kind of *off* to talk about plague."

Jessame shrugs. "Or the earth will get too close to the sun. The sun will die. A meteor will hit us. Something to do with space shrinking, growing, getting hotter or colder."

"But not for billions of years, right?" Lyss asks, directing her question at me rather than her sister. "Not for billions and trillions of years?"

Jessame rolls her eyes. "Who cares anyway? It's not like you can stop it. And at least we'd get out of our piano exams."

I am not really playing the game today. I'm not thinking of an answer. I play my own game instead, picking out objects with my eyes. A vase, a metal kidney-shaped hospital dish, a teaspoon.

At first I think Bonnie is not playing either, but it turns out she is considering her answer. "Definitely epidemic," she muses. "Some kind of cancer, maybe," she adds, with more scientific curiosity than self-pity. "You know that's what Tasmanian devils have? A sort of infectious, transmittable cancer?"

"What about you, Vega?" Lyss asks me. "How do you think the world will end?"

I shrug. "Maybe it already has. We just haven't noticed."

"*Don't,*" says Lyss. "I'll have nightmares." She pulls out a bag and carefully unfolds her knitting, a complicated white lacy blankety thing that she's making for some other cousin who's expecting a baby. They have lots of cousins. I have none, nor sisters or brothers. I only have Bonnie.

The next day at school. Lunchtime. The school smells of Vegemite-and-white-bread sandwiches, of pies with sauce, of freshly opened packets of BBQ chips. I go to the second-story bathroom in A Block. I lock myself in a cubicle, remove all my clothes, fold them, and place them on the toilet seat, with my shoes on top.

I used to spend whole lunch hours in here, hanging around inside a smooth gray river stone. I can enter any inanimate object, but I prefer stones. They are small and unremarkable, easy to carry around in my pocket in case of emergency.

Since Bonnie stopped coming to school, I've been experimenting more, discovering nuances in my power. I've learned I can travel from object to object without returning to my body. I slither into a brick, then to another brick, up and up until I get to the school roof, where I pour myself out, until I am in my own body again. The worst thing about my power is that I can't take my clothes with me. I have recurring nightmares about rematerializing in my own naked body in the middle of science class or PE. But on the roof of A Block there is no one to see.

I sit on the roof, hugging my legs against the cold pricking air, and look down on the schoolyard. The boys mostly play sports, or sit on the picnic tables, legs spread wide. The girls move in an elaborate dance, looping around the buildings, breaking formation, re-forming. And change your partners, *do-si-do*.

"They look so small, don't they? Like some kind of toy."

Vivian is standing on the roof beside me, looking down over the edge. I didn't hear her land, but she's so light on her feet this is no surprise. Vivian can fly. It's no secret. Some powers are too cool to conceal. I've never seen her on the roof of A Block before. Usually she is down there, in the thick of the dance, whirling lighter than air from one friend to another—clutching, laughing, now serious, now cruel—as if she invented the dance and it's her they are all trying to follow.

I am incredibly conscious of my nudity. It is the dream come alive, but as in my dreams, she doesn't seem to notice.

Not even really looking at me, she says, "You've got that sick friend, right?"

I nod.

"She gonna get better?"

Vivian is wearing a ring, gold with a pink jewel gleaming in it. "No," I say to the ring.

"Man," says Vivian. "That's so unreasonable."

She steps off the roof and free falls, until an updraft of air catches her. She lands lightly and joins the dance, never looking up to see if I'm still watching her. I heard she has hollow bones, like a bird.

"It's my turn," I say that afternoon. "If you could be any object you wanted, what would you be?"

"A bird," says Lyss, not looking up from her knitting.

"Nope," I say. "It can't be something living."

"It can't be technology either, can it, Vega?" says Bonnie, who is the only person in the universe who knows what I can do. "Nothing with a battery. No electricity."

"Shoot," says Jessame. "I was going to say my phone."

"What about an egg?" Lyss asks. "Is an egg a living thing?"

"It's, like, a chicken abortion," says Jessame.

Bonnie has the most scientific brain. "It's a cell from a living thing," she muses. "It begins its life with all the biochemistry to become a chicken if it's fertilized. There must be a point, though, where it crosses over and becomes inert. Like a blood cell or feces."

"Why would *anyone* want to be feces?" Lyss shudders.

"I'd be a condom," says Jessame.

"Ew!"

"What would you be then, Prissy Lyss?" Jessame challenges. "A wigwam for a goose's bridle?"

"Something beautiful," says Lyss. "Something intricate. Like a nautilus shell." Actually, it's a good answer. I think about twisting and turning down the corridors of a spiraling shell into its secret coiled heart.

"What about you, Bonnie?" I say. "What would you be?" But Bonnie has closed her eyes. She is no longer playing our game.

Lyss rolls up her knitting. Jessame shrugs herself back into her blazer.

"See you tomorrow," they say to me. They used to be my mortal enemies, appearing on weekends and holidays to take Bonnie away from me. I was jealous of the sinewy family ties that bound them to Bonnie, while my own connection felt alarmingly arbitrary, an accident of fate that deposited us in the same kindergarten class ten years ago.

After the sisters leave, I linger next to Bonnie's bed to say good-bye. Her eyelids are translucent; her skin has yellowed from being indoors so much, or from the medicine, or both.

"Vega," she whispers. "Don't go yet." She shuffles herself into a sitting position but begins to cough, an aggravatingly dry tickle that I can feel in my own throat. I reach for the buzzer to call the nurse, but she grabs my arm. "No," she gasps. She gives me the signal that means *private conversation*. We've been doing it since we were little kids, flashing it across classrooms or crowded playgrounds, behind the backs of boys, or at each other's dinner tables, right under our parents' noses.

I sit on the bed, waiting for the coughing to subside. Finally: "There's something I want you to do," says Bonnie.

Vivian sits next to me in math. She smells like atmosphere: sweet cumulus, savory sea breeze.

Mr. Smith walks into the room. "Open your homework books and we'll go through the answers."

I flip open my homework book, but I haven't even attempted it. I see Vivian hasn't done hers either.

"The thing is," Vivian murmurs, keeping her eyes on Mr. Smith, who is scribbling answers up on the board. "I know how I got up on the roof. But I wonder, how did you?"

It's not as though things were always perfect between Bonnie and me. We had a habit of falling for the same boys. Even girls would feel they had to choose between us. Some preferred Bonnie, who was funnier than me, and smarter, and kinder. Some leaned toward me, and to be honest, I have no idea why.

There was this one girl in primary school, Tammy, who made a sport of playing us off against each other in Year 5. I remember a particularly long tense afternoon of pretending to hate Bonnie in order to please Tammy, wildly flashing *private conversation, private conversation* at Bonnie when Tammy wasn't watching. I remember a different, rainy day, sitting on a beanbag in the reading corner, grimly holding back tears, while girls in the class gathered around, gasping breathlessly, "Aren't you and Bonnie friends anymore?" And Bonnie standing next to Tammy, staring blank-faced from the other side of the classroom.

Tammy was just one of those people who knew how to hurt you where it didn't show. She hurt you because she could, not for any other reason. She was like the cancer flourishing inside Bonnie. You couldn't even take Tammy personally. No point asking, "*Why me?*" Tammy was a bad thing that happened to good people.

When the bell goes for the next class, Vivian says to me, "My people usually hang out at the top oval at lunch. Why don't you meet me there and we can talk?" She's wearing her gold ring, the stone the dense, glassy color of raspberry ice pops. "It's a pink sapphire," she says when she sees me looking at it. She gathers up her books and leaves.

I don't go to the top oval. I spend lunch as a stone in the girls' bathroom. I haven't been going to the roof since Vivian found me there, in case she catches me midchange. I don't know what I look like when I'm changing, because I've never been able to change and watch myself in a mirror at the same time. Bonnie used to watch sometimes when we were kids, but we got shy about being naked in front of each other when we were about ten. Anyway, even if I didn't have to be naked, I'd still be embarrassed to have Vivian watch me do it.

"You know that phrase, making memories?" Lyss asks. "Well, if I was going to make a memory, I'd knit it."

"It depends on the memory," I say. Some memories are

still and certain; some are as alive and as impossible to catch in your hands as water.

"It depends," says Jessame, "whether you want to remember or forget."

"I'd draw on a blackboard. The most amazing, vivid, beautiful picture, my whole life in one big swirl," says Bonnie. "Chalk dust flying everywhere."

Lyss smiles.

"Then I'd rub it all out again," Bonnie says. We are all quiet for a minute. She asks, "What do you think will happen to them, my memories? I mean, what a waste. Don't you think? What's the point of them?"

Jessame walks out of the room. Sometimes it gets too much. Sometimes one of us just can't handle it, but we never break down in front of Bonnie.

"I'd knit it," Lyss says again. "I'd knit the whole history of human memory. And if I made a mistake, I wouldn't scrap it. I'd just keep knitting. I'd make the knots and holes part of the fabric."

Jessame comes back, pink around the rims of her eyes. She clinches Bonnie in a fierce hug and says, "Memories are old news, babe. Over and done with. Who cares? You can't hug a memory."

"You okay?" Bonnie whispers to Jessame and the question kills me. Jessame holds her and holds her.

"What color?" I ask Lyss.

"Black," she says, knitting. "With silver sparkles. Stretching out forever, like a night sky."

"I'd wear that," I say. "I'd totally wear that."

* * *

That night I think about the promise I made to Bonnie. I am not even sure if it's possible, if I'll be able to keep it. I get up, pad silently through the house to the kitchen.

In the ghostly light of the fridge, I hold an egg in my hands. At first it resists me, or perhaps I resist it. And then—*pop*—I am in. I *am* the egg: the shell, the phlegmy white, the rich yolk. The egg tumbles through the air, smashes against the lino, and I burst out, whole and sticky, the taste of it thick in my throat.

Words aren't objects. They aren't sturdy things you can shelter inside. You never know which conversation will be your last.

"What do you think happens after you die?" Bonnie asks.

"Heaven," Lyss says, with certainty.

"Boring," says Jessame, painting her toenails electric blue. "Everyone knows all the cool people go to hell."

"What do you think, Vega?" Bonnie says. She asks as if I might really know, as if all along this one was intended for me. But all I know is how to enter the cold, hard substance of a stone. I feel this makes me less qualified than anyone to answer Bonnie's question.

I shake my head, knowing I'm failing her.

"I think when you're gone, you're gone," says Bonnie. "The matter of you breaks up and is redistributed."

"What about your soul?" Lyss asks.

Bonnie shrugs. "An illusion of consciousness. Which is just brain activity."

"And you find that comforting?" Lyss asks.

"Not really. No."

But I do. I find the idea of Bonnie scattered through the physical world unspeakably comforting. I lean back in the vinyl chair, watching rain slide down the window outside.

I walk up to the bus stop after school. The road is shining wet, light has broken through clouds, and everything is rich with color. Vivian is at the bus stop too. She's not alone; there's a guy in a St. Francis uniform with her. He has blond, perfectly straight hair with a side part. He's the kind of guy Bonnie would fall for. Me too, once, but not so much anymore.

"Adam," Vivian says. "This is the girl I was telling you about. Vega, this is Adam. Adam's special. Like me."

Adam waves his hand, all false modesty. "Vivi is sensational. My talent is not so . . . *showy*."

Vivian flushes. I don't know if she has heard what I heard—a backhanded compliment, a dismissal of Vivian's power. It's hard to tell.

"I think Vega might be special too," says Vivian. She sees me looking at her ring and touches it gently, cocks her head, looks at me, sharp with curiosity.

Adam looks at me appraisingly, as if deciding whether or not to buy me or . . . or recruit me. His blond hair swings over one eye. "So *are* you?" he asks me. "Special?"

For weeks I've been harboring the same fantasy. "The thing is," Vivian will say again, "I know how I got onto the roof. But I wonder, how did you?" Instead of saying nothing, blushing with shame and secrecy as I did at the time, in my fantasy I turn to her and say, "I want to show you something. In private." We walk out of the classroom together and I take her to my toilet cubicle; we lock ourselves in together. In my fantasy, I ask for her ring and she hesitates. I say, "Do you trust me?" She slips it off her finger and puts it in my hand. My clothes fall away and the ring tumbles spiraling to the ground as I disappear inside it. Vivian gasps. She picks up the ring from my cast-off dress, and we (the ring and I) feel the heat of her spread through us. She slips her finger through us. She wears us down the hall, out into the air. Outside, she springs away from the ground, flying us up, up, and it is me and Vivian and a boundless curving sky.

"Are you special, Vega?" Adam asks me. I see the bus trundling down the road toward us.

"No," I say. I feel Vivian's disappointment seeping through her and into me, but I don't look her way. I say, "I'm not special at all."

Lyss calls me. She says, "We are all here, saying our good-byes. I know Bonnie would want you to be here too."

I enter that tight circle of family grief feeling like an intruder, but Lyss, who is holding it together, hugs me, and so does Jessame, who is not holding it together, and so does Bonnie's mum. "We've been here all day and none of us have eaten," she says. "We've all had some time alone with Bonnie. We're going down to the cafeteria. Do you want to sit with her? She specially asked me to let you, but you don't have to. Just if it feels right."

I nod tightly.

I enter the room and name the objects: chair, bed, teacup, water jug, Bonnie. I close the door behind me. I sit next to her and hold her hand. It feels cool and stiff, not like Bonnie at all. The blue polish on her nails has almost chipped right away. My jaw aches with the effort of not crying. I stand up and put my forehead to Bonnie's, put my hands on her face and will myself inside her, the way Bonnie asked me to do.

I will not cry yet. Later I will lie here, curled on the bed beside her, naked in my grief; only then will I allow myself the excruciating relief of tears. And later still that grief will make me strong, for this is only the beginning of what I can do and what I will be. All my life I will look for Bonnie in every object I enter. I will taste the salt of her in the marrow of the universe. I will listen for her voice in the whispering of things.

But for now, Bonnie is here, holding me with a promise, keeping me in this moment, for just a little time.

Now, into the substance of her, I descend.

Memory Lace

Payal Dhar

I can see myself in the mirror. There are soft curls falling to my shoulders, jeweled hair ornaments that catch the light if I move, beads that clink with every turn of my head. Only a soft, sheer veil separates me from the world. But it's a small world.

There is a rustle of canvas as the tent flap lifts and Veda ushers in another prospective buyer. A richwoman, well-rounded, prosperous-looking, clad in silks and silver. I'm guessing a landowner, or perhaps a merchant. She's trailed by a teenager. From the resemblance, I'd say daughter. The girl is about seventeen, the same age as me. Maybe her mother wants to buy me for her. I can hope.

One of Veda's assistants lifts my veil so the richwoman and the girl may lean forward to study the goods.

I have had a week's practice of blanking out at this point in the negotiations. Veda has never failed to find a buyer, but with just a day left before the fair winds up, I can see she's a little jumpy.

She's talking now in that deceptively low, soft voice she keeps for sales pitches.

". . . fine bone structure . . . rare this side of the Tapakoor Mountains . . . infallible pedigree . . ."

She makes a little sign with her hands, and her helpers turn my head first this way and then that. I fix my gaze upon the twinkling lamp near the tent flap and concentrate on it. There's a movement at my shoulder and a gasp escapes my lips as the cold strikes me. Veda's assistant steps back, letting the robe drop to the floor in a silky rustle.

". . . strong limbs . . . good posture . . . straight back . . . fine breeding stock . . ."

"I want to see the memory lace." The richwoman's sharp voice cuts through Veda's hard sell.

Veda beckons and a slender box appears in her hands. She opens it to reveal a velvet-lined interior on which lies a roll of fine white lace. I forget to breathe as the richwoman lifts it out and runs her fingers expertly over the intricate pattern. A shiver runs down my spine, but this time it has nothing to do with the chill air.

It's the fact that she has my life in her hands and, clearly, she knows how to read it. I don't know why they call it *memory* lace—it isn't just about the past. I asked Veda once and she replied that the future is just memories we haven't had yet.

I wonder what the richwoman reads about me. Does

it say where I was born? Who my mother was? What my skills are? When I will die?

What would happen if I were to lean forward, snatch it up, and throw it into the fire? Would that make me free? Or would I just stop existing?

Veda leads the richwoman to the table. The assistants pour drinks and serve sweets. The negotiations have begun.

A soft touch makes me start. It's the daughter. She has picked up my robe from the floor and put it back around my shoulders. I'm so startled that I look around and catch her eye. Nobody has ever done this for me before.

She looks back at me, head tilted slightly upward. Her eyes are frank, friendly. Not sizing me up, just looking. She smiles ever so slightly. Nobody has done that before either.

Her name is Fazal, the Grace of the Almighty. She is the richwoman's oldest daughter and now she owns me. I suppose I am privileged.

It is only after the long journey to her home that I am formally presented to her. I stand in the center of her day room as she approaches, and even though my head is bent down respectfully, I can see her coming closer in my peripheral vision. She puts a finger under my chin and lifts it. It is a curious gesture because I am taller than she is. It is difficult for me to keep my eyes modestly on my satin-sandaled feet.

For the second time in my life, I meet her eyes. The same open, genial look greets me.

"Do you have a name?" she asks.

I blush furiously. My sort don't have names till we are given them by owners; she should know that. "I used to have a number," I say.

"I see." She thinks for a while. "A number. I'll call you Sifar—zero, the number that means nothing, yet is the most important of all."

"You're too kind, Grace of the—"

She interrupts me. "When we are alone, you can call me Fazal."

Then she bursts out laughing at my startled face. I can't help smiling too, even though I don't know what the joke is. I just feel like smiling.

"Here." Fazal hands me a ball of yarn and a peculiar wooden implement, smooth and smaller than my palm. "This is a tatting shuttle. I want you to wind it for me."

She shows me how. There are a couple of small slits on the two ends of the shuttle, each leading to a larger hole. I wind the yarn so it passes through the slits into the holes. Soon the middle of the shuttle is thick with yarn.

"Like this?"

She examines it critically. "It'll do. Come sit here, I'll teach you how to use it."

I gather the folds of my flowing garment and sit cross-legged beside her on the cushioned bench. She leans forward on the table to consult a number of thick books. "Can you read?" she asks me.

"A little," I reply, looking doubtfully at the massive tome she is holding.

"All right, don't worry, I'll teach you."

She shows me how to wrap the yarn around three fingers of my hand and hold it closed in a circle with my thumb and index finger. Next she teaches me how to take the trailing thread with the shuttle in my other hand and pass it over and through the ring, pull tight . . . I blank out a little bit till she says, "There, and that's a double stitch. Now you try."

I blanch. "I . . . can't!"

"Of course you can. Even my little sisters can do it."

Two hours later, it turns out I really can. We laugh as we make colorful chains and little loops that she says are called picots.

I might go to the devil for saying this, but I think Fazal and I are becoming friends. The summer goes by and the days become shorter and cooler. Every evening at dusk, we lie on the grass, our heads touching, looking up at the sky.

"I read that there are machines that can take you up to the clouds," she says one day.

I laugh at the notion. "That would be flying. That's impossible."

"You should learn to read properly," she responds. "Then you'll be able to read the stories for yourself." She gets up and looks down at me. "We should start you on lessons."

"Then what about the tatting?"

She waves an arm carelessly. "You're clever, you can handle both."

I sit up. "Why are you doing all this?" I ask her. "All this playing around with threads and reading? One day you will run your mother's business empire. Don't you want daughters of your own?"

She looks at me curiously. "Of course I do." She studies me for a while. "Or maybe I'll have sons."

She gets up and runs inside. Her choice of words baffles me. Why would she want sons? Sons can't carry the family forward; they would be of no use to the business.

I meet Fazal's youngest siblings the next day. They are back from visiting their aunts for the summer. We are having a reading lesson when the door bangs open and two whirlwinds rush in.

"Sister! Where is it? Mother said we could meet—"

They come to a sudden halt in front of us. I can't help smiling at the pair of them. They are about six years old, too young to go away to school like their other sisters. They are twins, though they don't look much like each other. Their heads are shorn, like all girl children of upper families, and they're dressed in identical linen playsuits. Their eyes are green brown, like their sister's, and alive with mischief.

They study me with naked curiosity, as one nudges the other and says in a loud whisper. "Don't say 'it.' Mother says that's rude."

Fazal gets up and approaches them. They kiss her hand formally and then hug her tightly. I suddenly wonder if I ever had any sisters. Or brothers.

She puts an arm each around the two and turns toward me. "Sisters, this is Sifar." To me she says, "Meet Idraak, the Wisdom of the Ages, and Azaad, the Freedom of the Skies."

I bow to them. "I'm very pleased to meet you, Wisdom and Freedom."

"Idi," says the Wisdom shyly. She points to her twin. "And that's Aza."

"Sister, can we borrow your companion to play with?" Idi bounces up and down on her toes.

"No," says Fazal, catching the fidgety child by the shoulders. "We're working. You can work with us. Do you want to practice your letters?"

Aza, apparently the quieter one, but not at all shy, has come up to me. She fingers the curls on my head. "I love your hair," she says, and turns to Fazal. "Sister, do you think I could have curls when I grow up?"

Idi makes a face. "Curls are for boys."

"But I— '

"Enough," Fazal cuts in. "Get your books if you want to work with us."

One day Fazal asks me: "If you could have anything, do anything, what would you want?"

I think for a moment. "I want to fly—in those machines you mentioned that take you up in the sky." After a pause, I add, "And I want to wear trousers like you, instead of this ridiculous robe."

That makes her laugh. I like how I can do that so easily. She takes away the intricate pattern I'm tatting and puts a new shuttle in my hands. "Hold on to those thoughts about flying and trousers, and make me something beautiful."

That makes me laugh in turn. I can hardly hold the shuttle and yarn properly. It comes out uneven, but Fazal is inordinately pleased.

That night, after the evening meal, Fazal comes into my room. She holds a large parcel wrapped in brown paper, a smaller one covered in tissue, and a familiar wooden box. I have eyes only for the box.

I know that she owns my memory lace by rights, but I don't want to be reminded of it.

She must read something in my expression, for she comes close to me, puts her hands on my shoulder, and gently pulls me into a hug. "It's all right," she says softly in my ear.

I take a deep breath and force myself to calm down. I want to pull away and yet I don't.

After a few moments, she lets me go and hands me the larger package. "Open it."

Inside I find a pair of linen trousers and a matching tunic. A wide grin splits my face.

"Go on, try them on," Fazal says.

I do. They're a perfect fit.

"Can I wear them during the day?" I ask hesitantly.

"Of course. I'm having a couple of other sets made up so you have enough. Do you like them?"

"I love them. Thank you so much. I . . ."

"You don't have to thank me," she says, smiling at me as I jump and swing my legs about. The freedom of trousers is amazing.

I'm so happy; I rush over and give her a hug. But then, over her shoulder, I spy the wooden box.

"Why have you brought that?" I ask, dropping my arms and stepping back.

She lets out a long breath and looks at me in that direct way of hers. Without a word, she opens the box and lifts out the folded lace from it carefully. She holds it out to me.

I shrink back. "No!"

"It's your life," she says.

I shake my head. "It belongs to you."

She shakes her head back at me. "It belongs to *you*."

I expect a bolt of lightning to come down from the sky, tear through the ceiling, and strike her down for this blasphemous talk.

But the night is still as she lays the memory lace carefully on the bed. She then unwraps the smaller package. The messy lace that I made earlier in the day emerges from its folds. She takes it and places it in the purple-lined box in place of my memory lace.

"What are you *doing*?" My voice is raised in horror.

"This morning," she says, "you wove your dreams into the lace you were making. That's real memory lace. This"—she waves her hand at the lace on my bed—"is just something someone like Veda made to convince you that you have no control of your life."

For a few seconds I'm stupefied. "But . . . it's *written* . . ." I begin. Then it hits me and I fall silent again.

"All these months," I say quietly, "that's what you were teaching me? To weave . . ." I couldn't say the words. "*It*."

"Yes."

"But . . ."

"Oh, Sifar," Fazal sighs. She only says my name this way when she's frustrated. "You won't be the first boy that our family has freed. My father was a free man."

"But . . . there are no free men. All men are bound by the memory lace."

"All this palaver about memory lace—it's rubbish. Destiny isn't written. It's made."

A vice of fear grips me. "Are . . . are you sending me away?"

"No. But you are free to go if want to. Or you can stay—if you want to—as my companion or as my friend."

"I'm supposed to give you daughters."

"You're not *supposed* to," she corrects me. "It's something that both of us will decide, but in time. There's no hurry. There's so much we can do together, Sifar. I want to see the world. I've heard of places where men are treated like people. Don't you want to see that?"

My legs feel like noodles and I sit on the bed.

"If I can be free, does that mean Aza can have curls in her hair?"

"Yes." She pauses before adding, "*He* can."

Back- Stage Pass.

Who's there?

Soft you now— the fair Ophelia! What an *absolute* pleasure to have you here on *Back stage Pass!*

Wha— Who let you in here?!

You actually believe that I *wanted* to die?
I *told* him. I told him a hundred times that he wrote me all wrong.
I told him that if he'd just let me *speak*—

I'm an *actor*, remember?
Like the rest of them!
Do I have to spell this out??
I had a plan.
I was going to escape. Act crazy. Jump. Swim for it.
Get out of the unweeded garden for good.

But no.
The pen is mightier.
He pulled me down.
Drowned me.
Buried me.
And then he let them loose on me again, beating their chests and manhandling me in my grave.

Notes on the Collaborations

CAT CALLS
Margo Lanagan

Vandana Singh and I didn't really do much more than become Facebook friends and make alarmed noises about the deadline to each other. I wanted to write a story about an issue that concerned girls of both India and Australia, and "street harassment" was just coming to my attention as a term covering all those moments of public confrontation and humiliation that girls and women of both cultures endure. I also wanted to show girls doing something positive to confront the issue, and so I researched what action older women had taken and devised the collective gesture that my heroine and her classmates make. I hope this story doesn't look too much like wishful thinking.

SWALLOW THE MOON
Kate Constable

Having never worked with an illustrator before, I was very excited, but also slightly scared by the notion of collaborating with Priya Kuriyan in a graphic story. I didn't know what to expect, or how the process would work. What if I hated what she came up with? What if she couldn't stand what I wrote? While we exchanged our first tentative e-mails (and I sneakily checked out Priya's work online!), a vague image formed in my mind of a group of girls, walking silently through a dark forest. I sent Priya a very rough story draft, and when her first pictures tumbled into my inbox, I couldn't have been more thrilled. Her beautiful vision transformed a fairly dark piece of writing into something much more joyous and uplifting. The piece altered with each exchange, as Priya's illustrations became more detailed and I edited out more words. For me, the process of cutting the words, phrase by phrase, sentence by sentence, as Priya's work made mine redundant, was both confronting and wonderfully liberating. In the end, only about a quarter of my original draft remained, as together we built our story into something precious and filled with hope.

Priya Kuriyan

When I first read the piece that Kate Constable had written for the anthology, I literally got goose bumps thinking of how I would go ahead and illustrate the piece. There were paragraphs in her text that had such beautiful descriptions that I could immediately see the story in my head as I read along. I'm sure that if someone had peeked into my mind then, they would have seen a forest grow. I have to admit, it was also initially intimidating because I really hoped my visuals could match up to the beautiful prose. I had worked on collaborations with writers who wrote specially for comics before, but had never worked on a piece of long prose. I pondered a bit about how to go about it and it struck me that Kate had already "painted" these scenes through her words and I should perhaps look at four or five of these scenes and build the artwork around those key "paintings." Looking back, I'm myself quite surprised by the fact that, in all, the two of us must have exchanged only a dozen e-mails discussing the story before the piece came into being. Kate was incredibly generous and trusting, letting me interpret the story the way I ultimately did, and I do believe that is what the true spirit of collaboration should be. I feel incredibly lucky to have been partnered with her.

LITTLE RED SUIT
Justine Larbalestier

I grew up immersed in fairy tales, from the very first picture books that were read to me to Angela Carter's and Tanith Lee's retellings, which I fell in love with as a teen. The very first stories I wrote were fairy tales. (You can find one here: http://justinelarbalestier.com/blog/2009/03/18/the-toughies/.)

"Little Red Riding Hood" has been retold countless times,

but I always wondered why the hood was so important, so I decided to explore that question in a blasted hellscape future, with a red hood that was more of a spacesuit than a riding outfit.

Anita Roy and I came into this anthology late, so there wasn't time for a true collaboration. Had there been time I would have liked to have written an epistolary story with her, sending letters back and forth across continents, and possibly across time. We were, however, able to do a very useful collaborative activity: we read and critiqued each other's stories, improving them enormously. Thank you, Anita!

COOKING TIME
Anita Roy

Justine Larbalestier and I both came into this project—as writers—late in the day. I was at a writer's retreat at Sangam House just outside Bangalore, and she was over on the other side of the world in America, but it took only a couple of e-mail exchanges to realize that we shared the same sense of humor—the fact that one of Justine's books is called *Zombies vs. Unicorns* was a pretty good indicator of that! (And in case you're wondering: Zombies. Du-uh!)

The idea for my story came out of my obsession (shared by my eleven-year-old son, Roshan) with two TV series: *MasterChef Australia* and *Doctor Who*. But I soon realized that time-travel stories are an absolute nightmare to plot, because—in the immortal words of the Tenth Doctor—"People assume that time is a strict progression of cause to effect, but actually, from a nonlinear, nonsubjective viewpoint it's more like a big ball of wibbly wobbly, timey-wimey stuff." At various points, my sanity was rescued by excellent advice, not only from Justine, but from my coeditors, Kirsty and Payal. Without them, the plot would have disappeared up its own black hole, possibly causing a rift in the space-time continuum and destroying the known universe. It's a risky thing, this writing business. But, with fellow travelers like these women alongside to help steer, I am glad to be in it.

ANARKALI
Annie Zaidi

When we were first introduced over e-mail, Mandy Ord and I did not discuss any specific ideas. I was toying with "dystopia" but the worst I could imagine was already in the world—both our worlds!—which was hardly speculative. It was just depressing.

Then I was in Melbourne and meeting Mandy for lunch. We chatted about work, gender, etc. More friends joined us. I don't remember how we got talking about walls but I have a memory of the brick façade of the restaurant and saying something about walking through a wall. The very next thought was: Anarkali!

One of the great classics of Hindi cinema is *Mughal-e-Azam*, a film about Prince Salim (a historical figure, later a Mughal emperor) falling in love with Anarkali (a fictional character), who was walled up alive as punishment. The story has never ceased to trouble me and I promptly shared it with Mandy. We agreed that we wanted to shift the narrative—make her a rebel rather than a victim, focus on power rather than beauty. And then we were walking through walls.

Mandy Ord

I met Annie Zaidi briefly when she was visiting as part of the Melbourne Writers Festival. As our interactions after that became entirely electronic, it was wonderful to be able to place a three-dimensional person in my mind's eye when talking to Annie on the computer screen. I feel like this initial meeting made our collaborative process stronger, not to mention that the idea for our story originated from that one rushed lunch in a small Melbourne café.

During the meal and after much discussion, Annie was inspired to tell the tragic story of Anarkali, a young and beautiful Indian dancer from the Mughal period who was buried alive between walls during an ill-fated love affair. Annie told the story with such flair and passion that I was immediately fascinated. More intriguing was the notion that Anarkali may have been a real person and not just a character based on myth. It was an easy decision between us to chose Anarkali as our story and we delighted in the concept of reimagining a future for her.

Over many weeks and a constant flow of e-mails, Annie Zaidi and I researched and discussed ideas for the story structure, the visual language, and the notion of historical accuracy. I loved the collaborative process and was delighted with how rewarding it was to work with Annie.

CAST OUT
Samhita Arni

Alyssa Brugman and I started having a conversation about feminism and cultural differences. At the time of writing the story, I was very intrigued by how capitalism and consumerism had co-opted the feminist movement, and also by how technologies—like birth control—in the West had empowered women but in India had become a means of perpetuating gender differences, with even educated women choosing to abort girl children. (The economist Amartya Sen estimates that more than a hundred million women are "missing" in India.) I remembered listening, as a young girl, to a friend telling me that her mother had found herself pregnant with another girl and had chosen to abort the baby. We had then imagined an alternative life for that baby—and "Cast Out," in part, was inspired by that memory.

WEFT
Alyssa Brugman

Samhita and I were both interested in the interaction between feminism and consumerism. I consider myself a feminist, and I often struggle with the choices I make in my day-to-day life, and the ways I buy into a version of how women "should" be, or what our cultures tell us we should aspire to. This is what I wanted to explore in "Weft."

THE WEDNESDAY ROOM
Kuzhali Manickavel

"So you had never met before."

"No."

"And you live in India and she lives in Australia."

"Yes."

"Like, *MasterChef*, othersideoftheworld *Australia*."

"That's the one."

"And you've never written a graphic short-story type thing before either."

"Right."

"So let me get this straight. You got together with this person you'd never met, who lives in Australia, and you wrote a graphic short story together."

"That's right."

"Wow."

"I know."

Lily Mae Martin

Kuzhali Manickavel and I began e-mailing back and forth, but the story didn't form straightaway; distance made it hard for us to build up common ground to work from. But when Kuzhali began to have ideas about the story, the visuals came quite easily. I was really drawn to the dark and whimsical ideas of Kuzhali's story, and she was very clear what she wanted the main character to look like. Which is very helpful with a long-distance collaboration! I'm really excited about this story; it challenged me as an artist. I learned a lot about how to communicate the way I work, and how to put visuals with the words and words with the visuals.

APPETITE
Amruta Patil

The title of this anthology triggered instant synaptic activity for me. What does a gaping mouth look like with stars and galaxies and the components of our planet spinning inside? As it turns out, the image placed me deep in the turf of Indian mythology. The deity Vishnu and his avatar Krishna had both flashed their open mouths to reveal the multiverse inside—predictably causing much confusion and light-headedness among their audience.

Keeping the worlds-in-your-mouth idea, I decided to explore appetite—not gluttony or greed, but the desire to ingest life itself—through the eyes (and expanding form) of a young woman. Universally, the idea of appetite has been a gendered one. In stories old and new, feminine hungers are tame and measured; seldom does one encounter heroines with a large belly or tremendous appetite for food or, indeed, for anything else. Coral turns her oddness to advantage, and learns that the trick to make the most of living is not to hoard the goods, but to dissolve the outlines that separate you from the world around.

ARCTIC LIGHT
Vandana Singh

My ruthless work schedule prevented me from having more than a few early e-mail exchanges with Margo Lanagan. However, I have been an admirer of her work for a while, and that was certainly an inspiration to me as I went from a too-long first draft to an edgier, more realistically grim second draft. An Australian character in the first draft didn't show up in the final story due to space limits, but she is waiting patiently for her story to be told another day.

THE RUNNERS
Isobelle Carmody

I never much liked the idea of collaboration because I thought it would be all about having to compromise, but when Kirsty Murray sent me a link to the website of the illustrator she proposed to match me with, I couldn't resist having a peek. That was all it took to be blown away. Prabha is brilliantly versatile and amazingly talented. Dabbling in drawing in my own books has made me a lot more interested in artwork, and reverent when I stumble on someone who does it really well. So the thought of having Prabha draw my story was completely enchanting. I couldn't wait to see what she would come up with and I loved her illustrations enough to cut thousands of words down to a few, so that there would be plenty of room for her to spread her wings, artistically speaking. I feel absolutely honored to be able to work with her, and we are already plotting to collaborate again.

Prabha Mallya

Creating "The Runners" was a gradual process of working with a detailed futuristic world and characters with backstories, extracting from it all just enough to tell What Happened, with clues to the How and the Why and the

What If? for a dreaming reader to think about.

I imagine our collaborative process in its own special universe of time slowed to the speed of e-mails passed between a number of places in Europe and Australia, where Isobelle traveled; and the US, where I am.

A short description from Isobelle brought Hel and Geneva nearly fully formed into the world, and had us thinking and talking over what they look like, and where they live. The animals crept in, attracted to Hel in a mysterious way, having their own small roles throughout his journey. I drew scratchy cartoon people over Isobelle's scripts, she wrote and pasted over the drawings I made—each helping the other see what words could tell and how pictures could show. Isobelle started out with an abundance of words, bringing it to a trimmed final form; while I started with the barest of stick figures, building it up to detailed artwork. The very idea of a graphic story is words and pictures working together, and in "The Runners" they're inseparable!

THE BLOOMING
Manjula Padmanabhan
COLLABORATIVE WRITING, A HOW-TO GUIDE

The answer is very simple: be so lucky as to get Kirsty Murray as your partner. *grin*

Our method was to approach the project as a story-length version of the party game known to me as "Consequences," and to Kirsty as "Exquisite Corpse." We alternated writing passages of the story and, just to spice things up, we neither discussed the plot in advance nor any of the characters, setting, general theme . . . you get the idea? Yup. We flew blind into a hurricane of words and emerged with a story.

We also agreed to write it as a play. Why? Because one of the nice things about a script is that the writer can reduce descriptions to short, terse stage directions while the characters run amok, insulting one another, throwing tantrums, making up again, and spouting hot, tasty dialogue all the way. After the piece was written, we were able to trim away excesses, explain plot points, and remove confusions. Or try to, anyway! "The Blooming" is a wild ride and readers need to strap themselves in securely once the curtains open.

I am not at all interested in collaborations so I wasn't looking forward to it. I am grateful to Kirsty for making it so enjoyable. She's that rare person who can be warm and friendly, while also being really brilliant at everything she does. It was good fun.

Kirsty Murray

Working on "The Blooming" with Manjula made me realize that when you start weaving a story with someone, threads will connect you to each other across time and space, across oceans, continents, and cultures. I'd admired Manjula's writing for years, so when she suggested we play a writerly version of a game called "Exquisite Corpse" I was a little daunted. Would I be able to keep pace with such a formidably clever and talented author? Each of us wrote a section of the playscript without knowing the other's intent. We didn't discuss the story at all but sent each other a "surprise" section of the manuscript every few days, bouncing scenes, characters, and dialogue back and forth across cyberspace until the story had formed itself. The strangest thing was to discover that sometimes our thoughts were interconnected, even though we've never met. Symbiosis, imprinting, and clones aren't exactly mainstream ideas, but they came to us simultaneously and found expression in our collaboration. Truth is stranger than fiction, and every thought you conjure connects you to someone else.

WHAT A STONE CAN'T FEEL
Penni Russon

Writing is a social activity. Nowhere is this more obvious than on the Internet, where vast communities collaborate on giant living texts called Twitter and Facebook. One day digital archaeologists will sift through the jokes, trolls, micromemoirs, and haikus and make a picture of us—who we are in this time, in this digital shared playspace.

In the early stages of thinking about this anthology I played with the idea of "future" artifacts. Payal suggested we come up with an artifact that could appear in both our stories. We played word games, bouncing nouns and adjectives off each other and then putting them together. Rocking stone, wrong egg, floating sea, memory plot, imaginary sky, memory lace, fragile shadow, secret sky, fire edge, and wrong photo. We chose the one that resonated most strongly for both of us: memory lace. Both Payal and I had already thought about stories where two girls talked about their futures, so this became part of our projects as well. (The e-mails that Payal and I exchanged have become their own artifact, tracing the genesis of these stories.) I love that the stories are so different and yet share the same DNA, bubbling out of a shared playspace, negotiated across continents.

MEMORY LACE
Payal Dhar

Penni Russon and I were quite keen to base our stories around a unique artifact. So we took turns to come up with lists of five physical objects and five abstract modifiers, and then voted for our favorites to combine them into a really cool-sounding magical thing. "Stone dream," "wrong photo," and "secret sky" were all contenders, with Penni's daughters weighing in as well, till we decided on "memory lace." The other idea we were enthused about was to have two young women talk about their futures. It was hard to choose one idea, so we decided to be really wild and keep both (though I cheated a bit later on). Even though we started out with the same concepts, it was quite astounding how different our stories turned out. This was the first time I've worked with a writing partner. It was so much fun that I can't wait to do it again.

BACK STAGE PASS
Nicki Greenberg

Between 2006 and 2009 I worked on an enormous graphic adaptation of Shakespeare's *Hamlet*. Hamlet himself is a fascinating, enigmatic, and endlessly compelling character, and as readers we inevitably identify with his existential woes, his moral dilemmas, and ultimately his tragedy. But as I worked deeper into the play, I felt more and more strongly that the greater tragedy was that of his sometime girlfriend, Ophelia. Ophelia doesn't get many lines in this play. Instead we see this young woman berated and bullied by the powerful men around her, constantly told that her way of being is wrong, foolish, false, loose, dangerous. She absorbs these lessons so thoroughly that she loses all trust in herself, and even the ability to reason and act accordingly. Unlike Hamlet, Ophelia does not get the luxury of considering whether "To be or not to be." Instead she drowns in a stream, apparently having lost her mind.

"Back Stage Pass" is a sly way of giving a voice to the character of Ophelia. Not the voice of a victim, but the stand-up defiance of a young woman who rejects the role she's been given and is ready to make up her own.

About the Contributors
Indian Contributors

Samhita Arni is the author of *The Mahabharata: A Child's View*, the *New York Times* bestseller *Sita's Ramayana*, and *The Missing Queen*. Samhita is presently an impoverished writer, a full-time occupation that consists of waking up late every morning, having a bath once in two days, and consuming large amounts of espresso. She highly recommends it. samarni.com

Payal Dhar's flights of fancy help her seek out new life and new civilization in her novels for youngsters. She has written seven books and numerous short stories for both big and little people. She's also a freelance editor and writer, and writes about computers and technology, books and reading, games, and anything else that catches her interest.

Writeside.net

Priya Kuriyan is a children's book illustrator, comic book artist, and animator. Born in Cochin, she grew up in numerous towns in India. She has directed educational films for the *Sesame Street Show* (India) and the Children's Film Society of India. She has illustrated numerous children's books for many Indian publishers, the most recent one being *Monkey Trouble and Other Grandfather Stories*. She currently lives in New Delhi, where she mostly spends her time making (occasionally mean) caricatures of its residents in her sketchbooks, chasing pigeons, and singing tunelessly.

Priyakuriyan.blogspot.com

Prabha Mallya illustrates, writes, and makes comics. She can often be found drawing little cats, fish, and trees in her sketchbook, and frequently has black, inky fingernails. She has illustrated for *The Wildings* and *Beastly Tales from Here and There*. She crafts her own graphic short stories for various magazines.

Crabbits.wordpress.com

Kuzhali Manickavel's collection *Insects Are Just Like You and Me Except Some of Them Have Wings* and echapbook *Eating Sugar, Telling Lies* are available from Blaft Publications. Her new collection is *Things We Found During the Autopsy*.

Manjula Padmanabhan is an author, artist/cartoonist, and winner of the 1997 Onassis Prize for Theater. Her thirteenth (solo) book is on its way and she has illustrated more than twenty children's titles. She lives in the US and India for complicated reasons involving multiple families, a legalized male partner, and a fondness for solitude. She is a nonnurturer and professional sloth who never wants to cycle anywhere.
manjulapadmanabhan.com

Amruta Patil is a writer and painter. She is the author of *Kari, Adi Parva,* and *Sauptik,* and likes to tell stories using a sparky mix of pictures and words. Her work is often about mythology, living and dying, loving and eating, living in synchronicity with nature, and walking lightly on the planet.
Amrutapatil.blogspot.com

Anita Roy is a writer, editor and columnist with more than twenty-five years' publishing experience in the UK and India. Her stories and nonfiction essays have appeared in a number of anthologies, and she regularly reviews and writes for newspapers and magazines. She has completed her first children's novel, *Dead School.*
Anitaroy.net

Vandana Singh is a card-carrying alien from India, currently living in the US, where, as a professor of physics at a small university, she teaches about everything from quarks to climate change. Her stories have been published in numerous venues, including Year's Best anthologies. She is the author of the ALA Notable children's book *Younguncle Comes to Town*.

Vandanawrites.com

Annie Zaidi likes to write anything she can get away with. Plays, poems, stories, essays, reportage, comics. She is the author of *Love Stories # 1 to 14*, Gulab, and coauthor of *The Good Indian Girl*. She loves movies, especially the ones full of song, dance, and melodrama.

Knownturf.blogspot.com

Australian Contributors

Alyssa Brugman has written twelve novels for young adults. She recently completed a PhD in Narratology. She lives in the Hunter Valley in Australia and has a day job working with horses.

alyssabrugman.blogspot.com

Isobelle Carmody wrote her first book, *Obernewtyn*, when she was fourteen. It was accepted by the first publisher she sent it to. Since then she has written more than thirty books and many short stories, which have been translated and/ or won awards, including the prestigious CBC Children's Book of the Year Award. She has also written *The Cloud Road*, which she also illustrated; the Obernewtyn Chronicles series; and a screenplay of another of her books, *Greylands*.

Isobellecarmody.net

Kate Constable grew up in Papua New Guinea, where she spent her whole childhood reading. She has written ten novels for children and young adults, including the award-winning *Crow Country* and *New Guinea Moon*. She lives in Melbourne, Australia, with her husband, two daughters, a dog, a rabbit, and a bearded dragon.
Kateconstable.blogspot.com

Nicki Greenberg is a writer and illustrator based in Melbourne, Australia. Her first books, the Digits series, were published when she was fifteen years old. In 2008, Nicki's innovative graphic adaptation of *The Great Gatsby* was selected as a White Raven at the Bologna Book Fair. She then went on to tackle *Hamlet* in a lavish 425-page "staging on the page." *Hamlet* was joint winner of the 2011 Children's Book Council of Australia Picture Book of the Year award. Nicki has two young daughters who will be out-drawing her any day now.
Nickigreenberg.com

Margo Lanagan has been publishing stories for readers of all ages for more than twenty years. Her novel *The Brides of Rollrock Island* is a remodeling of the selkie myth. Margo lives in Sydney, Australia, just down the road from Justine Larbalestier.

Justine Larbalestier is an Australian-American writer of *My Sister Rosa*, *Razorhurst*, and the award-winning *Liar*. She also edited the collection *Zombies vs. Unicorns* with Holly Black.

Justine lives in Sydney, Australia, where she gardens, boxes, and watches far too much cricket, and sometimes in New York City, where she wanders about public parks hoping they'll let her do some gardening, and misses cricket a lot. Justinelarbalestier.com

Lily Mae Martin is a fine artist, writer, illustrator, drawing teacher, and blogger. Her work has been exhibited and published both nationally and internationally. She explores the relationship between art and motherhood, sexuality, anatomy, identity, and the domestic. Lily Mae has been shortlisted for the Rick Amor drawing prize and the Benalla Nude award 2014.
Lilymaemartin.com

Kirsty Murray eats too much chocolate but finds it helps her write. It seems to work as she's written twelve novels, many short stories, articles, nonfiction books, and millions of e-mails. Kirsty has been an Asialink Literature Resident at the University of Madras and writer-in-residence at the University of Himachal Pradesh. In 2012 she participated in the Bookwallah Roving Writers Festival and presented at literary events across India. Kirstymurray.com

Mandy Ord is a Melbourne-based cartoonist who has published numerous comic books and contributed stories to a broad range of literary journals and anthologies. Her book of short stories *Sensitive Creatures* was the recipient of

a White Ravens Award at the 2012 Bologna Children's Book Fair. She derives great inspiration from everyday life and the antics of her two small dogs.
Mandyord.blogspot.com

Penni Russon is the author of several novels for teenagers, including the luminous Undine trilogy (described by one reviewer as a "reading experience") and *Only Ever Always*, winner of the 2011 Aurealis Award, NSW Premier's Award, and WA Premier's Award for Best Young Adult Novel. Her books have been published in Australia and the US to critical acclaim. Penni has a Master's in Creative Writing, and as part of it she wrote a research paper on melancholy in children's literature. She is fascinated with the way fantasy and fairy tales can challenge cultural and generational gaps, transcending traditional notions of audience.
Eglantinescake.blogspot.com